THE MURDER RUN

THE TRAVELERS: BOOK SIX

MICHAEL P. KING

BLURRED LINES PRESS

Blurred Lines Press

The Murder Run

Michael P. King

ISBN 978-0-9993648-5-7

Cover design by Paramita Bhattacharjee at creativeparamita.com

The Murder Run is a work of fiction. The names, characters, places, and events are products of the author's imagination or are used fictitiously. Any similarity to real persons or places is entirely coincidental.

"King maintains his svelte, addictive style.... There's fresh tension here.... From the elegiac tone, readers may suspect disaster in the final pages.... The author alters the stakes in this entertaining con artist tale and brings his characters full circle."—*Kirkus Reviews*

Never cheat a partner. Always get revenge. . .

The Traveling Man takes on a quick and easy safecracking job...easy until his partners are murdered and he's on the run.

His wife is trying to settle into her new role as a rich man's girlfriend, so she isn't at his side.

Who are these killers who are after him? And how are they connected to the government agency that wants the envelope he took from the safe?

With the help of a new associate, he tracks the killers until he's steered into a trap. They think he's cornered, but he's still got one ace up his sleeve. . .

The Murder Run is a gritty, hard-boiled crime thriller. If you like criminal intrigue, surprising plot twists, and high-speed action, you'll love the sixth novel in the Travelers series.

Simply for Sarah

1

MITCHELLVILLE

On Wednesday, in Mitchellville, a few hours west of Washington, DC, the Traveling Man, a con man going by the name Tony Rogers, sat on the sofa, his head down, trying his best to look despondent. Janet Gibson stood in the middle of the living room, her hair wet, her Japanese robe pulled tight around her thin body, an exasperated look on her face. "We both knew this was coming," she said. "We've had some fun times."

He ran a hand through his gray-streaked hair. "More than fun."

"More than fun. But it's still over. Charles gets back from his deployment next week. And I've got a thousand things to do."

Tony sighed. He hoped he wasn't selling the emotion too hard. He really was sorry her husband was coming home. She liked a good time, she didn't ask too many questions, and she didn't have a lot of nosy friends or neighbors. This had been a great living arrangement. And even if he didn't want it to end, it was the best sort of ending. Her wanting him gone, not going all clingy because he had to make his escape.

He stood up. "You're right. We should make a clean break. We've had some great times, and that's the way I want to remember it. I'll be gone by the time you get home from work. I'll leave the key on the kitchen counter."

"Thank you." She crossed over to hug him. Her body was still warm from the shower, and she smelled of the shampoo he'd bought her. He smiled. If there was any goodbye sex in her plan, he certainly wasn't going to turn it down.

MISSY GREY SET her silverware down on her plate and sipped her wine. Where was Jerry Chen? She glanced past her girlfriend Betty, a tall, thin Eurasian in a tight dress, to the hostess station by the front door. He was supposed to meet them for lunch. That's why they'd chosen this vegan restaurant around the corner from his law office. That's why she was dressed for business in her usual men's suit and tie. She tried to hide her irritation, but Betty wasn't fooled at all. "Give him a call, sweets."

"No, it doesn't work like that. He asked to meet face-to-face."

"Then relax, enjoy the wine, and send him the bill."

Just then, Chen appeared in the doorway and rushed over to their table. "Jerry," Missy said, "I thought you'd be here in time for lunch."

"My apologies. My last meeting went long."

"You remember Betty?"

He nodded as he sat down. "I'm pressed for time. Can we get down to business?"

"Of course."

He lowered his voice. "I need documents taken from a safe."

"A real safe? Not one of those big-box store fakes?"

"A heavy wall safe. And there can't be any evidence of entry."

"That will cost you, my friend."

He shrugged.

"What are you willing to spend? Ballpark figure."

"Fifteen to twenty K."

"Okay, my end is two grand. I've got a guy in mind, if he's still in town. I'll give you a call today or tomorrow."

"Thanks." He reached into his pocket, thumbed through a wad of cash, and set some bills on the table. "That's for lunch. I've got to run."

Missy watched him zigzag off through the tables. Betty picked up the money and counted it. "Very generous."

"He called the meeting."

"Is this how one of these meets usually goes?"

"Usually. Unless they want to kill you. Which is why you always do the preliminary meet in a public place."

"Well, he certainly seemed nice enough."

"Yeah." Missy watched Chen pass the hostess station on his way out before she picked up her phone. This was curious business. Not like Chen at all. Paul Robertson would want to know about this. The phone rang twice.

"Yeah?"

"It's Missy."

"What can I do for you?"

"Isn't Jerry Chen one of your guys?"

"We're connected."

"He just asked me to find him a safecracker, an old-school touch guy."

"Jerry Chen?"

"Yep."

"He wants a guy who can open a safe without tools?"

"That's right."

The line was quiet.

"What do you want me to do?" she asked.

"Find the guy. And Missy, keep me in the loop. I'll drop three thousand in the usual account."

In Washington, DC, at the National Defense Agency, Paul Robertson glanced out the door of his office. He couldn't hear anyone in the hall, but he got up from his desk and shut the door just in case. Chen was a reliable guy and an excellent lawyer. He'd known him for years. He always stayed just on the legal side of the law, never crossed the line, which was why he'd recruited him for the Kyrgyzstan project. Jerry Chen? Hiring someone to crack Clemens's safe? It just didn't make sense.

Robertson went to his window and looked out on the park across the street. People were sitting on benches eating their lunches out of paper bags. The trees were in flower. The grass was green. How could anything be going wrong on a day like today? The plan was simple. He dealt with the intelligence angle from here at the National Defense Agency. Chen did the legal paperwork. French and his contractors took care of the Kyrgyzstan end. Clemens did the back-and-forth from his spot at the embassy. Everything nice and tidy. But when the others found out what Chen was up to, all hell would break loose. Chen was his guy. He had to find out what was really going on. He took out his cell phone.

"Jerry? It's Paul."

"You're not supposed to call."

"And you're not supposed to be breaking into Clemens's safe."

"Clemens's safe?"

"Don't deny it."

"I'm not crazy, okay? I'm not trying to steal from the group."

"Then what are you doing?"

"Three guys are dead since last month."

"That's overseas."

"I think French and Clemens are reducing our numbers to increase their shares."

"You're paranoid."

"Easy for you to say. You and French are old buddies. But he doesn't need me anymore since the last green card came through for the Kyrgyzstani nationals."

"So what are you planning?"

"I'm going to get the bank-account codes and put them some-where safe. Then when French and Clemens get here, and I'm still alive, we can access the bank account together and make the split."

"Jerry, don't break into Clemens's safe. When French finds out, I won't be able to protect you."

"Paul, that's the whole point. When I have the bank codes, I'll be the only one who can access the numbered account. I won't need protection."

"You're making a mistake."

"Don't worry. I'll be untouchable once I have the codes. Everything will be fine."

"You've never seen French go ballistic."

"You're not going to change my mind."

"Okay, then." Robertson ended the call.

He turned off the lights as he left his office. Chen was fooling himself. If French found out that he was planning to steal the bank codes to the numbered account, he'd have him killed in a minute, police investigation or no. And they couldn't have police involvement, not now, not when they were so close to splitting up the money. Maybe he should call French, try to spin Chen's actions before this situation careened out of control. He punched the button for the elevator. No, that was a stupid idea. If he backed Chen, French would think he was part of Chen's plan. He could call Missy and make sure that Chen couldn't get a safecracker. But then what would Chen do? Reach out to someone unreliable? Put the project at even more risk? The elevator door opened. No, the best thing for him to do was stay out of the way. Chen thought he could handle things. Maybe he was right. If not, it wasn't his fault. He'd tried to warn him.

CLARA GARCIA CAUGHT sight of Robertson as he ambled down the hall to the elevator. She knew he was dirty. She'd been leading the investigation into the Kyrgyzstan foreign aid scam for over a year. They'd turned Clemens, a state department employee stationed at the Kyrgyzstan embassy, almost six months ago. So she knew that Robertson was running interference from this side while an NGO contractor and Kyrgyzstani criminals were skimming the aid over there. Clemens had emailed her that the scam was closing down and the principals were coming to the US to make their final preparations to divide the money. This was the tricky point. Events were moving at high speed. It looked as if the conspirators were turning on each other, killing anyone who was no longer needed, but Clemens had managed to get control of the only copies of the bank-account codes and had placed them in the safe in his home office, which was why, in all probability, he was still alive. Her team had to stay focused. They needed to keep Clemens's apartment and Robertson under surveillance. The bank-account codes were the key. When the contractor and Clemens showed up, her team needed to be ready to seize the codes and take all the conspirators into custody.

On Friday, Tony sat in a black RAV4 in a parking spot in front of Chen Associates, a law office among a strip of professional offices located near a cluster of restaurants. He was waiting for Missy Grey, a player he knew who'd called him about a possible job. And there she was, coming down the sidewalk, in her men's clothes and athlete's swagger. He got out of his SUV and buttoned his suit coat to hide the Glock on his hip. She spotted him and waited.

"Trav," she said.

"It's Tony Rogers now."

She nodded. "Where's your wife? I don't think I've ever seen you alone."

"She's busy elsewhere."

She pushed open the door, and he followed her in. A google search had told him that Chen was a fiftyish Chinese American who specialized in green cards, visas, and international contracts of various sorts. The waiting room was dark paneling, heavy furniture, and Impressionist prints. The receptionist, a middle-aged woman wearing a sweater set and pearls, looked up from her computer.

"We have an appointment," Missy said.

She nodded. "Go on back."

Chen's office was more of the same, but law books and diplomas replaced the artwork. Chen stood up from behind his desk to greet them. He was a lanky man in a black suit. "Have a seat," he said.

He gave Tony that evaluating look all lawyers seem to learn in law school. "Don't tell me your name. I don't want to know it. Missy vouches for you. That's all that matters. Will you do the job?"

"Fill in the details."

"It's all straightforward, really. The apartment owner is out of town indefinitely. In his home safe—this is a real safe, not some discount-store fireproof box—is a manila envelope and a bag of diamonds. You bring me the envelope, unopened, to my house. You keep the diamonds and anything else you find. I give you five thousand dollars when you hand me the envelope. Most important, there must be no sign of intrusion—nothing broken, no witnesses, no police, no disturbance of any kind. That's what I'm paying for."

"This is blackmail material."

"Yes."

"They can't run to the cops when they find out it's gone?"

"Whenever he finds out, he can't go to the police."

"When do you want this job done?"

"As soon as possible."

Tony studied Chen's face. "Five thousand dollars is not much money."

"For a few hours' work? If the job is done right, there's no shooting, no police, no getaway."

"But I'm the one who makes sure the job is done right. I need to get paid. How do you know the diamonds are there?"

"They're there."

"If they aren't, you kick in another ten thousand."

"You could take the diamonds and claim they weren't there."

"And you could call the cops after I give you the envelope. Trust has to begin somewhere."

"Okay," he said. "An extra ten if the diamonds aren't there."

"It's a deal. Do you have the job details?"

Chen passed him an envelope. "Address, safe specs, everything you need to know. When will I hear from you?"

"Monday unless there's a glitch. I'll scout it out, hire my help, get it done."

"But anyone you hire will know nothing of our arrangement."

"Their arrangement is with me."

LATER IN THE AFTERNOON, Tony sat in the Caffeination coffee shop across the street from 2087 Cummings Place. It was a ten-story red brick apartment building with a doorman. The safe was six floors up. He counted three security cameras that were easily visible. There were sidewalks down both sides. He'd walked the block. Dumpsters and parked cars lined the alley behind the building. Two more cameras guarded the service entrance. The fire escape on the side of the building, on the other hand, might be an access point. The fire doors would be alarmed, but the roof access? Unlikely. He thought about climbing up and climbing down without being seen. That could be a problem. The easiest way would be going through the front door. He sipped his coffee. The plan still needed a lot of thought, but he knew he needed two guys to work this job. Who did he know who was close at hand? He'd seen Duke in a bar on Kellogg two weeks ago. This was his kind of gig. Duke was a large black man who had a face like a TV preacher. Civilians believed anything that came out of his mouth. Plus he was good at picking up vehicles, equipment, uniforms—he had some sort of union connection. Maybe he had a friend. Tony got out his smartphone.

"Hey, Duke, you working?"

"No."

"You still here in town?"

"Yeah."

"I'm moving, need two guys to help with the lifting. You interested?"

"Yeah."

"You know a guy?"

"I've got someone in mind."

"Great. Can you meet me at the Cup-N-Sup over on Grant Avenue tomorrow at eleven a.m.?"

"I'll be there."

Tony drank some more coffee. This little project was hardly big enough to be called a job. Bag of diamonds and five grand—split three ways, maybe as much as $6,000 apiece. Not vacation money. But it would pay the bills. He should call his wife, Nicole, and fill her in. He didn't think he'd need her help, but she'd want to know. She was semiretired, living with James Denison, a millionaire they'd helped out of a scrape. It was her retirement package: the easy life, hanging out in San Francisco drinking martinis. It was a work in progress.

"Hey, honey."

"Tony. How are you?"

"Never better. Got some work lined up."

"Need any help?"

"Not worth a plane ticket. Missy Grey turned me on to it. Duke and a player to be chosen are going to carry me across the goal line."

"You know you can't trust her."

"I'm not trusting her. I'm trusting my plan and my team."

"Holler if you need anything."

"You know I will. How are you?"

"Bored. The straight life—every day is the same. There's nothing to do."

"No shopping? No late lunches? No going out in the evening?"

"You know what I mean. No challenges. Every day blurs into the next. I hate to whine—I know that this is what lots of people hope for, but the money spends better when you have to steal it."

"It takes a while to adjust."

"I don't know if I want to adjust."

"It's always easy to see the downside of your current situation. How many slobbery fat guys have you had to fuck lately? How many times have you been shot at? You've got to focus on the positive."

"I may have made a new friend."

"Really?"

"I snuck off to a hotel bar the other day to flirt some free drinks—you know, just to keep my hand in the game—and there she was, hustling two business dudes. She reminded me of me back in the day."

"She was working alone?"

"Yeah. She's just a kid, really—doesn't even know she's on the con. She's just playing."

"Well, have all the fun you want, but don't start picking up strays. If she digs herself into a hole, walk away."

"I'm a big girl. I know how to take care of myself."

"Don't we all. I'm just saying that you and Denison come first."

"And what about you? You got this project sewn up?"

"Me? I've got Duke watching my back. I've never seen him hesitate when push comes to shove."

"You're going to make me jealous."

"Please. Remember when that guy was going to stab me and you tackled him? He had you by a hundred pounds."

"Didn't make any difference. I got your back."

"That's right," he said.

"I love you."

"And I love you. Watch yourself."

"You too."

PAUL ROBERTSON STOOD at his desk. His briefcase was packed. His desktop was clear, and his desk was locked. Weekend getaway in the mountains. Regional quilt show and bluegrass convention. Phase one of his save-my-marriage program. The marriage counselor had said that with the kids out of the house, they needed to get back to basics. He couldn't expect the kids to keep Martha company; it was up to him to work on their relationship, and that meant taking the time. Retirement was looming. He didn't want to lose her, didn't want to be that lonely guy eating cereal for lunch. If he could just do enough to keep her from leaving until he had the retirement money set. His extra cell phone buzzed in his pocket.

"Robertson?"

"Yeah?"

"It's French. Can you talk?"

"I can listen."

"Chen is planning on cheating us."

"I don't believe it."

"I've got him bugged. He's having Clemens's safe robbed."

"He must think something crazy is about to happen. I'll talk with him."

"We're past that."

"Why?"

"If there was a problem, he should have called. He didn't. He's proved he can't be trusted."

Robertson lowered his voice. "You can't just drop bodies on US soil."

"Relax, I'm on my way to you. I'll send some guys to deal with him."

"This isn't what we agreed."

"There's only a few loose ends left. I'm not letting them ruin the plan. Either a guy wants to play it straight and take his cut or he gets cut out. I'm not being cheated by anyone."

"We don't need to draw any attention right now."

"Don't worry. There'll be plenty of misdirection."

"From your guys? I'm going down to Mitchellville to make sure everything stays quiet."

"Suit yourself. I'll be in touch."

Robertson slipped his phone into his pocket. So much for the weekend getaway. *Just look the other way for old times' sake. Provide a little intel. Get the money you need to pad out your retirement.* That's what French had told him in the beginning. Every step of the way, the danger had increased. Now French was planning to kill Chen. In the US. What a clusterfuck. He was dancing in the middle. The dead guys in Kyrgyzstan didn't matter. French and his mercenaries, Clemens, Chen, and he were playing musical chairs with the envelope containing the bank-account passcode. All that mattered was being in a chair when the music stopped. If Chen had the bank codes, that was fine. If French had them, no problem. But if French killed Chen and the cops discovered their plan, he'd lose his pension and wind up in prison. There'd be no way to finesse his way out of it.

So he was going to have to run down to Mitchellville. Protect his investment. See if he could find a way to keep Chen from being killed. Nothing could be left to chance at this stage in their plan. He reached for his desk phone and called home.

"Martha?"

"Let me guess. You have to work this weekend."

"I promise this is absolutely the last time."

"That's what you always say."

"I'm doing everything I can. It's not my fault when I draw the short straw."

"I'm not going to be held hostage by your job. I'm going to the mountains. And I'm going to see if Meagan can go with me, so don't bother to call me every day with your sad story about how you're on your way in a few more hours."

She hung up. Robertson tapped the phone handset against the edge of his desk. Six months until retirement. He'd get this deal done, get the money ferreted away, increase their mortgage payments, pay off the credit cards, and they would be set. He'd make it all up to her. They'd go on those cruises she always wanted to go on. Spend time with the grandkids. Go to Europe. In a few years, she'd forget all about how hard things were now.

2

THE WINDUP

On Saturday, when Tony came into the Cup-N-Sup in Mitchellville, the place was full. It was breakfast all day, and the waitresses were scurrying back and forth with plates of pancakes and specialty omelets. Tony squeezed up through the line at the hostess station. Then he noticed Duke motioning to him from a booth at the back corner. Duke's friend was sitting with his back to the wall. He was a skinny, freckled-faced guy wearing a shoulder rig that he wasn't hiding in his jacket very well.

"Hey, Tony," Duke said. He half-stood to shake hands. "This is Barker." Barker didn't shake. He just lifted a hand and nodded.

Tony slid into the booth next to Duke. "You guys been here long?"

"I got a friend here," Barker said, "so we didn't have to wait." The kitchen door swung open and smacked into a cart of dirty dishes. Barker jumped.

"Don't worry," Duke said. "I've known Barker a long time. He's not jumpy when he's working. Damn good driver. Where's your woman?"

"She's not on this one."

"I guess there's a first time for everything."

Their waitress, a sturdy middle-aged blonde whose hair needed a touch-up, appeared at the booth. She smiled. "What's it going to be?"

Tony glanced at the others. "You going to eat?"

They shook their heads.

"Bring me some coffee," he said. "And don't you worry. We're going to take care of you for using your space during the busy time."

She slipped her pad into the pocket of her apron and turned away.

"So what gives?" Duke asked.

"This is a little one-off deal. Break and enter. About fifteen thousand split three ways, maybe more."

"Sounds good."

"The hitch is this—"

He paused while the waitress set his coffee down in front of him.

"We're stealing blackmail info, so there's no cops if we get away clean, but there might be blowback. So if it's not for you, now is the time to walk."

Barker shook his head. "I need the money, bro."

"You line up the job," Duke said, "I'm always in."

"Great. It's a doorman building. Security cameras and the whole nine yards. Can you get us some sort of service van, uniforms—you know the deal—plus an extra car?"

"For Monday?"

"Yeah."

"No problem."

The waitress came by with the coffee pot. Tony waved his hand over his coffee and stuck out a twenty-dollar bill. "Keep the change."

THAT EVENING, Nicole and James Denison were in the bedroom of their condo in San Francisco. He was standing in the walk-in closet looking in the full-length mirror to tie his necktie. He was tall and thin with a neatly trimmed beard, in excellent condition for fifty-seven years old. She was sitting on the bed in yoga clothes, watching him. Ever since she'd gone to visit him at his Florida house, she'd been playing what she thought of as the honesty con, making him love her while only telling him the truth. It was a difficult con because true intimacy was an aphrodisiac that worked on both players in the game. It had been a long time since she had had to pretend that she loved him.

"You look great," she said.

"Come to the fund-raiser. Everyone asks about you."

"You know I can't go anywhere where my picture could be taken."

"Dye your hair. Change your makeup. No one will recognize you."

"Until the cops come with the handcuffs or somebody looking for payback comes knocking at the door. And then you're in the papers or shot as collateral damage. We're not going through this again. Private groups only. At least for now."

"We're not done talking about this." He glanced at his wristwatch. "I'll be back before midnight."

"I hope the auction is a big success."

"Thanks."

She walked him downstairs to the front door. A rideshare Lincoln was sitting at the curb. They kissed. She watched him get into the car. As she shut the door to the condo, her phone pinged. It was a text message from her new friend, Lily. She opened it. *Can you play? I'm at Tracy's Piano Bar just north of the convention center.*

She leaned back against the door. Tony was right. She needed to be careful. A chance encounter with an old mark in Cricket Bay had turned into a fiasco. Almost gotten Denison's daughter, Bell, killed. But she couldn't turn her world into a prison to avoid trouble. She'd been on the grift her entire life. Living involved risk. Staying out of the limelight was an obvious precaution. But some anonymous action in a dark bar? Caging some free drinks. Lifting a married man's wallet. What was the harm? She texted back: *On my way.*

After Nicole changed into a clingy party dress, she took a cab to Tracy's Piano Bar. A throng of conventioneers, many still sporting their name tags, filled the tables and crowded the space around the bar. She could barely hear the soft jazz emanating from the back. She scanned the faces, looking for Lily, when she felt a hand on her elbow.

"Glad you could make it," Lily said. She was a twenty-four-year-old petite blonde with a dazzling smile. She wore a tiny frock that left little to the imagination.

Nicole leaned over to Lily's ear. "How did you find this place?"

"I work at a travel agency. This is a nice, safe, business-professional bar."

"A few of the women are probably working girls."

"You mean prostitutes?"

Nicole nodded.

"How can you tell?"

"Because they're dressed like us, and all the other women are dressed for success."

"I never thought of that," Lily said.

"We need to manage expectations. What's our backstory?"

"You tell me."

"We work at Kaiser in accounts payable. Boring. Don't want to talk about it."

"Got you. See those guys sitting in the comfy chairs by the wall?"

Five businessmen of various ages sat with drinks in their hands and envious looks on their faces as they watched the crowd. "The wolf wannabes?" Nicole asked.

"I've had my eyes on them for a while. They seem pretty safe."

"Let's get some free drinks."

WHEN DENISON GOT BACK to the condo at 1:00 a.m., he found Nicole sitting in the den in her pajamas. A black-and-white movie was playing on the TV.

She smiled. "Hey, handsome."

"What are you watching?"

"I'm not sure, really. I just turned it on."

"I'm surprised you're still up," he said.

"I haven't been home that long."

"Where did you go?"

"I was out with Lily—you know, that girl I met a couple of weeks ago. We had some drinks."

"Have fun?"

"Yeah. She always cracks me up."

"You know, she's one of the few people you've met since you came here. You should invite her over some time." He untied his tie.

"How was the fund-raiser?"

"Too many people to talk to. But the auction went great. Samantha Hegland and Norma Roland were a big help."

Nicole added a little purr to her voice. "I'm sure they were."

"Nicole, really—"

"Jimmy, you're by far the most eligible bachelor in your world. And you're fun and good-looking. It would be surprising if there weren't some women sniffing around."

"I'm not interested in other women."

"I'm just teasing, Jimmy. I know what kind of man you are." She used the remote to turn off the TV. "Let's go to bed."

SUNDAY MORNING IN MITCHELLVILLE, Robertson sat in a Ford Explorer on the street three houses down from the craftsman-style bungalow where the Chens lived. There was a For Sale sign in the yard of the two-story brick house he was parked in front of. Three of the houses on this block were still quiet. Two vehicles, a Suburban and a Toyota Sienna, had pulled out of driveways loaded with kids dressed for soccer. At three other houses, occupants had taken in newspapers off the lawns. Now a guy was starting to mow the lawn behind him. He slid down in his seat. He'd already placed transmitters in the Chens' cars. As soon as they left, he'd place them in their living room and kitchen. Used to be easier in the old days, when you could just bug the landline phones, but those days were long gone.

After he got done with their house, he'd head over to Chen's law office. Chen had admitted he was going to take the bank-account codes, but Robertson had to be sure there wasn't more to his plan. Chen was definitely afraid that French planned to kill him, but that didn't mean he hadn't gotten greedy. There was a lot of money involved. And since French had Chen bugged, Robertson wanted to know what French knew as soon as he knew it, not when he decided to tell him. Because French and Chen were right about one thing—with the project winding down, no one could be trusted until the money was divided and the numbered bank account closed. And even if French was an old friend and definitely wouldn't kill him, he was a loose cannon. His war-zone ethics were going to land them all in prison if Robertson couldn't stop him from creating complications.

THAT AFTERNOON in the San Francisco Bay Area, Nicole and Lily stood off to one side in an event room at the Bridgewater Club. A wedding reception was in progress. Guests were milling about, drinking champagne and eating hors d'oeuvres that were being served by the waitstaff. The bride and groom weren't yet present, but the three-tier wedding cake sat on a covered table near the band, which was playing some innocuous pop music. Nicole set her empty glass on a side table. What was she doing here? When she'd called Lily, it had all seemed so innocent: A few laughs, some free drinks, the pleasure of convincing some strangers that they knew her from somewhere. But now she heard the Sirens singing, and she couldn't seem to resist. "Do you want to play a game?"

"What kind of game?" Lily asked.

"Have you ever lifted a man's car keys?"

"That's the game?"

"No. Guessing what the keys go to before you lift the keys, that's the game."

Lily got another glass of champagne from a passing tray. "Let me get this straight. We choose a guy. Guess what car he drives. Pickpocket his keys. Find out if we're right."

Nicole nodded. "So back to the first question. You ever lifted a man's keys?"

Lily giggled. "How hard could it be?"

"You want me to go first?"

She shook her head. "Pick the guy."

"See the guy in the seersucker?"

A potbellied, balding man wearing a seersucker suit was talking with a younger couple. The woman had a definite baby bump under her dress. "A Cadillac," Lily said.

"Lexus. Cadillac isn't flashy enough. Keys look to be in the front right pocket."

Lily downed her drink, clutched the empty glass in both hands, and circled around to the other side of the group. Just as the woman turned, Lily staggered into Seersucker as if she was on part one of a lost weekend. The glass hit the floor. She gripped Seersucker's jacket by the lapels. He stumbled backward. Her hands were all over his front as she tried to get to her feet. Finally, the young man got her shoulder and steadied her.

"You okay?" the pregnant woman asked.

"Never better," Lily slurred.

She zigzagged off toward the ladies' room. Nicole followed. Out in the hall, Lily dropped her act. She held up Seersucker's keys and jingled them. "Got the car fob and the house keys."

Nicole laughed. "You are insane."

"It's not a Cadillac or a Lexus." She held up the fob.

"Porsche."

They walked out of the club and into the parking lot. Lily clicked the fob as they walked along. The lights on a red Porsche Boxster flashed. "So what do we do now?" Lily asked.

Nicole felt the old excitement. "It's a beautiful day for a ride in a convertible."

Lily's mouth fell open. "Steal the car?"

"We're not stealing it. We're just going for a ride."

"We're bringing it back?"

"Of course. He won't even know it was gone."

A group of teenagers in suits and dresses came out of the club and started across the lawn, getting louder as they moved away from the building.

"I thought I was the wild one. But it's pretty obvious I was wrong," Lily said.

"Ride or no ride?"

"Let's do it."

"Give me the keys."

THE ROBBERY

Monday evening, Tony sat with Duke and Barker in a stolen Arnold's Pest Control van across the street from 2087 Cummings Place. They were all wearing latex gloves and blue coveralls with names sewn over the chest pockets. Just as a UPS truck pulled up in front of the apartment building, they climbed out of the front of the van, opened the back, and pulled out a two-wheel cart loaded with pesticide spraying equipment. Duke grabbed the handles on the cart. Barker shut the van doors.

Tony pushed in his earpiece. "Keep a sharp eye out."

"I got you covered," Barker said.

Tony and Duke rolled through the front doors of the apartment building just as the UPS woman was unloading her second cart of boxes and the doorman was checking them against a computer print-out. "Where's the service elevator?" Duke asked.

The doorman raised his hand. "Hold up. Where you going?"

Tony looked at a clipboard. "602."

"Let me check on that."

They kept moving.

"Hold your horses."

Duke rolled his eyes. "You want your residents to see us?"

"Give us a break," Tony said. "This is our last job. We want to go home."

"You signed off?" the UPS woman asked the doorman.

The doorman signed the UPS tablet. "Okay," he said to Duke and Tony without looking up. "Service elevator is around to the left."

"Great," Duke said. They started away.

"Wait a minute," the doorman said. "602 is out of town."

"Yeah," Tony said. "We got keys. They want it done before they get back."

In front of apartment 602, Duke watched the hall while Tony picked the locks. Easy-peasy. They turned on the lights. The apartment looked like it belonged to a bachelor—wall-to-wall carpeting, leather furniture, framed posters of horse races. In the spare bedroom/home office, the safe was in the wall behind a framed U2 poster. "What do you see?" Duke asked.

"No challenge here."

Tony had the safe open in a few minutes. Inside were a few file folders and, as advertised, a sealed manila envelope and a small cloth bag. He tossed the bag to Duke. Duke shook some of the contents out into his hand. He grinned.

"What have we got?" Tony asked.

"Diamonds. Small. I'm guessing fifteen thousand cash."

Tony shut the safe and rehung the U2 poster. They turned off the lights and locked the door on their way out. Duke gave a wave to the doorman as they came out into the lobby. Barker opened the back of the van as they were crossing the street. "All good?" he asked.

"Never better," Tony said.

Up the street half a block, a National Defense Agency operative sat in the back of a Suburban looking at a computer monitor. Four days of surveillance had finally paid off. She'd recorded the two men up in the apartment, plus she had silent footage of the van on the street. The street lighting here really was excellent. And she'd had enough time to compromise their smartphones by channeling their cell phone signals through a fake cell tower. You just had to love the way people left their phone GPS tracking on. She called Garcia.

"Ma'am, a crew just broke into Clemens's. They were in and out of there like they owned the place."

"What did they take?"

"They took an envelope and a small bag from the safe. Do we move on them?"

"Is the tracking up?"

"Yes, ma'am. We're inside all their phones. I've taken over the Find My Phone feature, and we'll have all their data downloaded in four or five hours."

"Excellent. Let them roam. I want to know which of the conspirators they're connected with. Call up Ridley. Transfer the surveillance to him. Tell him I want a complete profile on these guys as soon as possible."

BARKER DROVE the van out onto the beltway going north, took the next exit, and doubled back south. The traffic was light, mostly semi-trucks. No one was tailing them. He took the third exit onto Mission Drive and second right onto Rockhaven Road. A Toyota Camry sat under a broken surveillance camera in a high school parking lot. They put their coveralls and gloves into a garbage bag before they climbed into the Camry. Barker drove back onto the beltway, drove south to the last exit into town, and got off on First Avenue, where he pulled into a half-empty strip mall parking lot and stopped beside Tony's RAV4, which was parked in the far corner of the lot.

"You guys hold the diamonds," Tony said. "I'll meet the client, collect the five thousand, and meet you at your place."

"We'll dump the Camry and get rid of the garbage bag," Barker said.

"And I'll call Fats about selling the diamonds," Duke said.

Tony parked on the street in front of Chen's house, a story and a half in a neighborhood of picket fences and well-tended lawns. It was still early, before 7:00 p.m., but the street was quiet. He walked up onto the porch and knocked on the front door. No answer. He found the doorbell and pressed it with a knuckle. He couldn't hear any movement inside. He used his handkerchief to grab the doorknob. The door swung open. "Chen!"

He pushed the door shut with his foot. There was something—something in the air, a scent that made his back teeth tingle. He pulled his Glock and quietly chambered a round. He held his gun out, military style, working his way step by step toward the back. Off to his right was a hallway. The first door was the bathroom. The door was open. The shower was running, but the shower curtain was torn down. A dead woman, Caucasian, maybe fifty, lay in the tub, her blood swirling down the drain. She'd been sprayed with bullets. Now he remembered what the smell was. Gunpowder and blood. He listened as hard as he could, but all he could hear was the spray hitting the tub.

He continued down the hall to the kitchen. Chen lay in the floor between the counter and the kitchen table. Dead. His face was bloody, as if someone had worked him over before they shot him. Tony looked out the back door. The yard was peaceful suburbia. He turned back into the room. That's when he saw the white, business-size envelope on the floor under the table. He picked it up. Five thousand dollars cash. Must have fallen off the table during the struggle. He slipped the envelope into the right-hand pocket of his jacket. He glanced back down at Chen. The blood was still wet. In a neighborhood like this, if there was gunfire, someone would call 911. It was time to go. Tough luck for Chen. But he had the money and the diamonds, and maybe he could off load the blackmail information, so all in all, a good day's work.

Outside, there was a man leaning against his RAV4 under the streetlight, a nondescript man with a regular haircut wearing a dark suit that screamed federal agent. Tony glanced up and down the street. There was no one else. A dog barked in the distance. Tony kept the Glock down along his leg as he came off of the porch.

"Good evening," the man said.

"Who are you?"

The man held out his identification. Paul Robertson, National Defense Agency.

Tony nodded. "So you're not a cop."

"No."

"You're working late."

"I need that envelope."

"What envelope?"

"Don't play fuck all with me. The envelope from the safe."

"You been in the house?"

"I was too late. They obviously didn't know you hadn't arrived yet."

"Or they would have waited." Tony smiled. "Unless it was you."

"Please. I didn't need to kill the Chens. The first mention of rendition to a black site, and I would have had their full cooperation." He stuck out his hand. "The envelope."

Tony unfolded the manila envelope out of his inside jacket pocket and handed it to Robertson.

Robertson glanced at the writing on the outside. "Thanks."

Tony got into his SUV. Only God knew what was really going on there—why Chen had him steal the envelope—but it didn't matter now. He had the cash and the diamonds. He pulled away from the curb. Still no sirens. But why was Robertson conveniently waiting there to collect the envelope? Had Robertson been following him, or had he been trailing the bad guys?

Just to be on the safe side, Tony drove around town for a while, stopping at a Gas N Go and at a Caffeination coffee shop. No tail. Then he drove down Mercer Boulevard to the freeway interchange where he and his partners had agreed to rendezvous at The Sundowner Motel, a rattrap at the end of an access road. The motel sign flashed on and off in the dark, and a few old cars sat in the parking lot. He pulled in next to the Ram truck parked in front of room 125. His headlights showed that the door to the room was ajar. He knew that he should just drive away, but he had to know for sure. He got out of the RAV4 with the Glock in his hand. He stood behind the wall next to the door and pushed the door open with his foot. No gunfire. He stepped into the room and flipped on the light switch. Duke was lying across the first bed, shot in the head and the chest. Barker was lying facedown by the bathroom door.

Tony bumped the room door shut with his shoulder. He needed to move fast. He slipped on a pair of latex gloves. He flipped Barker over. One in the head, two in the chest. Execution style. He went through Barker's pockets methodically. Nothing. No cash, no wallet, no car keys. Duke was the same. But Duke was old school. He would have hidden the diamonds first thing. Tony pushed Duke to the floor and lifted the mattress. Nothing. He hurried into the bathroom and looked in the toilet tank and under the sink. Ditto. He felt the undersides of the dresser drawers and the bedside tables. No luck. He stood in the middle of the room and turned full circle. The diamonds weren't here.

He shut the door behind him. This was the second time he had arrived between the bad guys and the cops. How many minutes did he have? He started toward the RAV4, but the Ram truck just sat there, inscrutable and alone. What the hell? He picked the lock on the passenger's side and popped open the glove box. There it was. The small cloth bag. He snatched it up, swiveled his head around like a cartoon character expecting the large hammer, and jogged over to the RAV4.

He began to feel safer when he got off the freeway two exits south. Who were the killers? Definitely professionals. Rogue law enforcement? Black ops? Drug cartel? The envelope from the safe obviously didn't just contain some blackmail info. Think. The guys that killed Duke and Barker couldn't have known about the rendezvous. They must have been waiting at the break-in. So why did they follow Duke and Barker instead of him? But the guys who killed the Chens knew where they lived and knew they were going to get the envelope. They just got there too early. So did they double back to the apartment building after they killed the Chens? Was it just plain dumb luck that they had followed Duke and Barker instead of him? Or was Robertson the key? And if it was Robertson's crew, why was he alone at Chen's? If it was some other crew, were they still looking to grab the envelope? Tony drove downtown until he saw the sign for a long-term parking lot.

He pulled into the long-term parking, wiped down the inside of the RAV4, and left the keys in it. Did the bad guys think Duke and Barker had the envelope, or were they just cleaning up? Why didn't they wait for him at Chen's? They were going to kill everyone anyway. He opened his rucksack and pulled out a set of shanked keys. A white Nissan Sentra was parked under the second level, safe and dry. He slipped his Sentra shanked key into the door lock and gave it a turn. He was inside. He shoved the key into the ignition, gave it a jiggle while he turned it. The Sentra started on the first try. Half a tank of gas. He took his smartphone from his pocket. Robertson—the government guy—had been waiting at Chen's. Either he was rogue, or it was a straight-up government operation. Which meant his phone was probably compromised. He went into his contacts and wrote down Missy's and Nicole's phone numbers. Then he went into Settings, erased the contents and settings on the phone, and pulled the chip. As he drove out of the parking deck, he tossed the phone and then the chip out the window.

He drove to a Mail-N-More at a strip mall where he kept a PO box, put the diamonds in an envelope, and put the envelope in his box. The middle-aged Latina behind the counter didn't even look up from the box she was packing. Then he went to a Save-U-Mart, where he parked across the street at Ted's Liquors so that the Sentra wouldn't be on the security cameras, and purchased a cell phone. When he got back to the car, he called Missy.

"Hello?"

"Do you know who this is? Don't say my name."

"Yeah."

"Throw away your phone."

"Why?"

"'Cause your phone might be hacked. Remember where we first met?"

"Yeah."

"Meet me there."

. . .

MISSY LAID her phone down on the seat of her car. Tony didn't do drama. What could have gone so wrong? It was just a simple little job. The cops get after them somehow? A civilian get killed? Damn. She was going to have to find out. She drove across town to The Fishing Hole, an old-timey bar on a corner in a rundown neighborhood. She hated bars like this. It was dimly lit and smelled of floor cleaner and old beer. It was the kind of place where lonely old men went to die. Three guys sat at the bar, all by themselves. Tony wasn't one of them. She motioned to the bartender. "I'm looking for Chuck."

"He left this note for you."

It was a phone number. She went to the pay phone in the corner and dialed it.

"Is this a new phone?" Tony asked.

"Pay phone."

"My guys are dead. Meet me at Parkside Apartments, number 302."

"What's this about?"

"Come or don't come. I'll be waiting there two hours."

She went back out to her car, sat behind the wheel, and looked down the street. The stoplight changed from green to yellow. His partners were dead. This wasn't some random nonsense. She got out her smartphone and called Robertson.

"Missy, how are you?"

"I don't know. The safecracker's guys are dead. That wasn't part of the deal."

"Settle down. I didn't have anything to do with that. Some people got their messages crossed."

"I thought you were in charge."

"I am now."

"Really?"

"You're still alive, aren't you? We've got an ongoing relationship. You've got nothing to worry about. Go on home. Everything is fine."

"You sure?"

"Absolutely. You're on my team."

Missy pulled away from the curb. Robertson had always had her back. Ever since he had made those robbery charges go away and recruited her to find criminals to do projects for him, his word had always been good. He got what he wanted, her friends got paid, and she made her finder's fee, which meant she had to do fewer cons to support her own lifestyle. A big win for everyone. Robertson was insulated from the crime, her criminal friends were insulated from Robertson, she got paid for standing around. She took a right turn at the four-way stop. But now? This job had developed too many moving parts. It didn't look like Robertson was calling the shots. It looked like he was coming afterward with the dustpan and broom. And his assurances just weren't that convincing.

She pulled into a driveway and turned around. This was no time to take chances. She needed her go bag. With killers on the loose, the smart move was to give Robertson a few days to smooth everything out. If he could. She speed-dialed Betty.

"Baby, where are you?"

"I'm at the gallery. Remember? Tonight's the reception for new clients. I won't be home until late."

"Don't go to the house."

"What are you talking about?"

"You need to stay away from the house."

"Are the cops coming? Are you going to be arrested?"

"No. And I don't want you to worry. Go to your brother's."

"He's going to ask why."

"Tell him we had a fight, anything, just don't go to the house."

"Tell me why."

"It might be nothing. Right now, you need to do what I say."

"I need clothes."

"Run in and run out. Don't even turn on the TV or use the bathroom. If anyone is sitting in a car on the street, don't stop."

"You're scaring me."

"Good. You should be scared."

"When will I see you?"

"A day or two. I'll be in touch as soon as I can."

"I love you."

"I love you."

TONY WATCHED Missy turn around in the driveway. He pulled over to the curb and ducked down in his seat as she drove by him. Then he made a U turn and followed her three cars behind. She was easy to tail. He followed her to a townhouse, watched her come out with a large shoulder bag, and followed her to the Parkside Apartments. He was in the hallway behind her when she rang the doorbell to apartment 302.

"Hey, Missy," he said.

She pivoted, reaching inside her jacket, but dropped her arm when she saw who it was. "How long have you been following me?"

"Long enough to know that nobody else is. We cool?"

"Yeah, we're cool."

"Then let's get inside."

He opened the door with a key. No one was home. Janet was at her book club, and her husband wasn't due for two more days.

Missy sat down on the sofa. "Nice-looking place. Whose is it?"

"Old girlfriend."

"So what happened?"

"What do you know?" Tony asked.

"I hooked you up. Chen reached out to me, I reached out to you. I've done work with him before. What did he have to say?"

"When I got to his house, he was dead. His wife as well. A Fed was waiting for the envelope."

"Jesus Christ. So a federal guy takes the blackmail envelope, and your guys are dead when you go to meet them?"

"That's about the size of it."

"No disrespect. I'm sorry about your guys. But why can't we walk away?" Missy asked.

"How deep is this problem? Between the cash and the diamonds, I earned—what? Twenty K that nobody cares about? So that envelope must be worth at least ten times that. That isn't some run-of-the-mill blackmail info."

"But that doesn't matter. The Fed has the envelope, right? So we just need to lie low for a few days."

"But do the bad guys know that? They're going to keep coming 'til they have the envelope or know we don't have it. Or maybe they're just tying up all the loose ends," Tony said.

"So you want to hit them first?"

"They got it coming. Nobody gets away with killing my partners. A few minutes earlier, I could have been with them in the motel room when those assholes showed up."

"But you weren't. You've got twenty grand. All the rest is just speculation."

He gestured toward the door. "You think you're safe, you can walk away. No hard feelings."

"I didn't say that. I'm just saying we don't know very many actual facts."

"You're right. We need a computer jockey. Somebody we can trust."

"Don't you know somebody?" she asked.

"I'm not getting any of my people involved until I know the lay of the land."

"You're just talking about a researcher, not a scammer?"

"Yeah."

"I know a woman. She dabbles in the game, but she's not on anyone's radar. Let me give her a call."

Shortly after 11:30 p.m., Tony and Missy were sitting in office chairs around a small round table in the home office of Missy's friend Joan, a middle-aged woman with short dark hair whose T-shirt and camp pants were wrinkled from bed. A desktop computer sat on a height-adjustable desk against one wall. Family pictures hung above it. They all had coffee cups in their hands.

"Okay," Joan said, "you got me up. What can I do for you?"

Tony leaned forward. "We need to know everything you can find out about a lawyer, a federal agent, and an apartment, particularly anything that links them."

"So we're talking phone records, work records, property records, and anywhere they lead?"

"Yeah."

"And you couldn't call tomorrow?"

"I assume you don't want to know what you don't want to know."

"So it's that kind of job." She looked down at the table and ran her finger around in a puddle of spilled coffee. "I'm done with all that. I don't need the extra money anymore." She looked up at Tony. "But I can do this favor for you if you can do a favor for me."

"I'd rather just pay you," Tony said.

She shook her head. "Favor for favor."

"Maybe we find someone else."

She glanced from Tony to Missy and back. "Good luck. Sorry you wasted your time. I was just thinking since you're under time pressure we might help each other."

"Let's just hear what she wants," Missy said.

"Okay. What have you got in mind?"

"My step-daughter—she's a grown woman now—she got on drugs and fell down the rabbit hole. It took her a while, but she lost everything. Couldn't keep a job. We did the tough-love thing. Just made things worse. Now she's being whored out of a drug house."

"Selling herself?" Tony asked.

"Being sold. I went there to get her back, take her to rehab, but this big guy just laughed at me."

"Why don't you call the cops?"

"Because I don't want her in jail, and I don't want those thugs after me."

"So you want us to get her out of there?"

"Yeah."

"You don't care how we do it?"

"No."

Tony set his coffee cup on the table. "Won't make any difference. She'll run back as soon as she gets loose."

"I have to try."

"You have to try. Okay, we'll help you out. Get this info for us, and as soon as we're squared up, we'll get your daughter out."

Joan shook her head. "You get my daughter first. If I help you first, you could just walk away."

"So could you."

"No, I know your kind. You'd kill me if I welshed."

"So we work at the same time. You get started on our problem while we get started on yours."

"I can do that."

"Have you got a recent picture of your daughter?"

Joan took a picture off the wall and took it out of its frame. "She's the one in the middle."

Three young women sat on the steps of somebody's house. The middle one was a skinny blonde whose face already had the innocence worn out of it. "What's her name?"

"Sylvia."

"What's the address of this drug house?"

Joan wrote an address on a scrap of paper.

"You sure she's still there?"

"Yeah. She's there." She pushed a legal pad across the table. "I really appreciate this. Write down all the information on the targets, and I'll get started."

At 2:00 a.m., Tony and Missy sat in a stolen Toyota Corolla hidden in the on-street parking across an intersection from a row of three-story houses in the dilapidated neighborhood just south of downtown. Two large white guys sat on lawn chairs on the porch of one of the houses. Cars drove up, men got out and talked to the guys on the porch, then bought drugs and drove away, or were admitted into the house.

"Just like Joan said," Missy said.

"And they're not worried about a thing."

"How many guys do you think are inside?"

"Two or three. The crew leader and the dope guy, maybe another gun. I bet the women are on the second or third floor," Tony said.

"So we're screwed."

"We're not going in the front. We can't win a straight-up gunfight."

"Then what's the plan?"

"The houses on either side are boarded up. How wide do you think those alleys are?"

"You might be able to squeeze a smart car down them."

"Let's have a look at the back."

Missy turned left at the intersection and drove around the block. She pulled to the curb between two broken-down single-story houses. There was a car parked in the driveway of the left house, but both houses were dark. "Can you see the back of the drug house?"

"Yeah. It's all boarded up."

"So no way in," Missy said. "Look, I'm armed. I've shot people when I had to, but running and gunning? This is out of my league. How about if we sneak back there and set the house on fire?"

"They'll pull the drugs and money. They won't care about any women." He rubbed his chin. "But the alleys—drive up around the corner."

They parked on the street half a block south. "We've been thinking about this wrong," Tony said. "We don't have the muscle for a rescue. But maybe we can pull off a burglary."

"A burglary?"

"Yeah. We're going to steal a woman out of that building. Let's see if we can get in through the roof."

They crept down the sidewalk, staying in the shadows, until they came to the abandoned house to the right of the drug house. The plywood was hanging loose on a side window, and a bucket sat upside down underneath the window as if someone had used it for a step. They pulled the plywood aside and climbed in. Tony held a small flashlight down toward the floor as they moved along. The first floor of the house was broken plaster, filthy carpet, and food trash. A stained mattress lay in the dining room. Bits of foil, squares of paper, and broken syringes were scattered about. Up on the second floor, the bedrooms were nests. Old sleeping bags and blankets were piled into the corners. The third floor was the same.

"Nobody," Missy said.

"Drug crew must have run off the squatters."

They found the roof access stairs. Tony pushed the door open and peeked across the flat roof. No one was up there. He crawled out. Empty beer cans and liquor bottles littered the roof. He gazed over at the drug house's roof. It looked like a party spot. There were a circle of lawn chairs, a gas grill, and a couple of coolers. He motioned to Missy. They walked over to the edge of the roof.

"So close," he said.

"Look," she said, pointing to her right. "They've got an extension ladder."

"Insurance policy so they don't get trapped up there."

"Think we could jump?"

"Too much noise."

He glanced about the roof. An old TV antenna lay on the far side. The pole was ten feet long easy. He carried it back to Missy. "Okay. I'm going to lay this pole across the alley. You're going to hold this end while I shimmy over. After I collect Sylvia, we'll use the extension ladder to get back."

"That's crazy. You think a stoned addict is going to crawl across that gap on a ladder?"

"You got a better idea?"

She sighed. "No. But instead of you crossing over on the pole, I'll get in the car. Drive by. Fire some shots at the front of the house. You jump over while I'm firing."

"You sure you want to do that?"

"I'm not running up the steps; I'm driving by. It'll catch them off guard. By the time they're shooting, I'll be gone."

"Okay. It's your neck."

He walked across the roof to the street side and waited. When he saw the Corolla turn the corner, he jogged down to his starting spot. She started firing. The guys on the porch fired back. He ran, jumped the alley, and rolled across the roof of the drug house, barely missing the gas grill. The gunfire stopped. He crept over to the roof access door and tried the handle. It was locked. He picked it. He eased the door open and listened. He could hear voices, but he couldn't make out what they were saying. He tiptoed down the steps to the third floor. The voices were louder, but he still couldn't make out the conversation He pulled his Glock. He eased open the closest door. The room was empty. So were the other two. He stood at the top of the stairwell. Someone was talking. He sat on the steps and slinked down step by step. Finally, about halfway down to the second floor, he could make out what was being said.

"Fucking john bitching," one voice said.

"Lucky we didn't cap him just to be sure," another voice said.

"Boss said to move in case the cops show," a third voice said. "Who's got the back?"

"Jimmy's back there. It's clear. Red has the front. We're good to go," the second voice said.

"Start the car," the third voice said.

"What about the girls?" the first voice asked.

"Are you kidding? They'll find us," the third voice said.

He heard footsteps and the front door open and close. He crept down to the second floor. The nearest bedroom was empty, except for a bare mattress, a box of condoms, and some used syringes. Out the window, he saw the drug crew pile into a Suburban and drive away. This rescue had become a lot easier than he thought it was going to be. In the next bedroom, a skinny dark-haired woman lay passed out on a mattress, naked, her underwear bunched up by the pillow. He looked at the photo of Sylvia. It wasn't her.

He opened the door to the third bedroom. There she was, her dress twisted up around her waist, glassy-eyed, drool running down her chin. She was supposed to be twenty-three. She looked like she was forty and that she'd gotten there the hard way. He jerked her dress down. He couldn't find her panties.

"Hey," he said.

Her head began to move.

"Wake up."

She looked at him, but her eyes couldn't seem to focus.

He pulled her to her feet. Her legs started to buckle, but she found her footing. He put his arm around her waist. "Sylvia. Walk."

She stumbled along as he helped her down the stairs and out the front door. Missy was parked at the curb. Tony laid Sylvia on the back seat and then climbed into the passenger's seat. "Good job," he said.

"I didn't expect them to run."

Missy put the car in gear, sped down to the first corner, and took a right. "She's a mess. Should we get some Narcan?"

"Why? So she can be sober and angry? She's a lot easier to deal with right now. And there's no risk of her running away to find a fix."

"I was just thinking of Joan."

"She needs to see what she's got."

"So long as her daughter doesn't die on us."

Missy took a left at the next intersection, drove two blocks, and doubled back into the downtown. Then she drove out to the freeway, sped past two exits, and dropped onto a boulevard by a Walmart. "Nobody's following us."

"Excellent."

The sky was tinged red in the east. They drove back to Joan's house, taking it easy, pulled up in the driveway behind Joan's Prius, and walked Sylvia up the steps to the front door. "My God," Joan said.

"This is the way we found her," Missy said.

Tony let Joan take his side. Joan and Missy led Sylvia down the hall. Tony wandered into the kitchen, rummaged through the cabinets until he found a bottle of vodka and a glass. He didn't really care for vodka, but what the hell. He poured two fingers. Then he went back into the living room and glanced out the windows. The day seemed fragile. But there was no one suspicious on the street. They were safe for now. At least they hadn't added to their problems.

Joan stood in the doorway. "I see you've made yourself at home."

He shrugged.

"You can sleep on the sofa. I'm making progress, but I've still got a ways to go."

"Okay," he said. She turned away. He got out his cell phone and called a number he knew.

"What?"

"It's the Traveling Man."

"New phone."

"It's been one of those days, or I wouldn't be calling now. I'm going to need an insurance policy."

"Got you covered."

"I'll be in touch later today."

4

NEXT STEPS

In the early morning in San Francisco, Nicole woke to birdsong and city traffic. She slipped out of Denison's arms in the dark and padded across the carpet to the bathroom. When she got back, his eyes were open.

"Hey, honey." She slipped back into bed and cuddled up against him. "How was your sleep?"

"Didn't wake up at all. You?"

"Fine." She laid her head on his shoulder. "What's on your agenda today?"

"I'm not sure. I think I'm at the office most of the day. We need to find more space for the after-school program. Jill has some meetings lined up. How about you?"

"I don't know. Lily will probably call."

"You're spending a lot of time with her."

"You jealous?"

"I just don't know what to make of it. She's the first friend you've made since you've come here—if she is a friend."

"You're a peculiar boy." She propped herself on her elbow to look him in the eye. "I never know what's going to get your Spidey senses tingling. I've got a confession to make. This straight life is harder than

I thought it would be. Cricket Bay was like a long vacation, and then I had to win over Bell, which was sort of like running a con, and then everything went crazy. But now, in your real life, I don't have a place here. I'm just hiding out."

"I know you're struggling. You need to find something to do that gives your life meaning."

"That's what you keep telling me, but it's easier said than done. I've got my old patterns. And that's where Lily comes in. We've been going out to night spots, flirting free drinks. Anonymous and innocent enough. No chance of getting into trouble. But then on Sunday, we crashed a wedding, and..." She paused for a moment. "Took a car for a joy ride."

"Took a car?"

"I couldn't help myself. I knew it was too much risk, that if I got caught there'd be real repercussions, for me as well as for you, but rolling down the highway, the wind in my hair, I felt so alive. Even putting the car back was a real thrill."

"So you stole a car, drove it around, and then took it back?"

"The ultimate grab and drop."

"And you didn't get caught?"

"No."

"After all the times you told me that you had to be careful. That you couldn't risk being seen."

"I know it was a mistake."

"A mistake?" Denison sat up against the headboard. "I'm an honest guy. I believe in ethics, morals. What do you and Tony call people like me?"

"Civilians."

"Yeah. I'm a civilian, and I'm proud of it. In Cricket Bay, with everything on the line, I let my morals go relativistic. Don't get me wrong. I'm not sorry I did it. You got Bell back. But I can't live like that. For normal life, there's a right and a wrong. And I want to do what's right."

"I understand."

"Do you? I know I agreed that you could go help Tony when he needed you, but you're going to have to find a way to leave that life behind when you're here with me."

"I know. I'll find a way to make it work. I'll find something to do. I promise."

"We could go away somewhere. Be on vacation until you find your way."

"But then you'd have to give up your work. You couldn't do that long term. Besides, what would your kids say?"

"Bell and Skip aren't running my life. We can do whatever we want."

"It's more complicated than just being one place or another. Just give me some space to work this out."

"Okay." Denison put his hand on her shoulder. "But no more secrets."

"No more secrets."

BACK IN MITCHELLVILLE, it was midmorning by the time Joan came into the living room carrying a cup of coffee and a file folder. Tony sat up from the sofa and stretched his arms overhead. "Here," she said, handing him the coffee.

"Thanks."

She sat down facing him. She looked worn to the bone. Her eyes held that fearful look of a person who was carrying a psychic load that was too heavy to bear. He needed to do what he could to give her a few strands of hope to hold on to so that they would be well in the wind before the crash and burn of the futile plan to save her daughter. Instinct told him to start personal, let her share. Missy walked in, her shirt untucked and her suit coat over her arm.

"Coffee's in the kitchen," Joan said.

"I don't drink it in the morning," Missy said.

"How's your daughter?" Tony started.

"She's still asleep."

"She's in pretty tough shape. You got a plan?"

"I thought—I don't know what I was thinking. She looks a lot worse than I thought she would."

"But you're doing the right thing. Looks like you got to her just in time."

"I hope so."

"Can you get her into a program today?"

She shook her head. "I know someone. I've been planning for this, but it will be tomorrow or the next day at the earliest."

Missy saw what he was doing. She knelt next to Joan and took her hand. "So you've got to keep her from running. You get that, don't you?"

"Yeah."

"Only two ways. Lock her up until you can get her into detox. Hope she doesn't get too sick. But she's an adult—she doesn't have to go. The other choice is to get her some dope and talk her into rehab."

"Buy her dope?"

"Just enough to keep her level until your spot opens up. Your decision. You do what's best." She got a card out of her pocket and wrote a number on the back. "This guy isn't an asshole. He'll treat you right if that's what you decide. Methadone, heroin, whatever you want."

"Methadone?"

Missy nodded. "Might work if she wants to clean up and you catch her before she's too shaky."

Tony picked up the thread. "I know that you want to focus on your daughter. So you want us out of here, right? What have you got for me?"

"I've got everything you asked for." She glanced in the file folder. "The lawyer Chen is a real lawyer, and the NDA guy—Robertson—is a real NDA guy. The apartment? It belongs to Rodney Clemens. He's a state department guy who's stationed at the embassy in Kyrgyzstan. He's been back and forth four times this year. Mother in the hospital. Mother's funeral. Two other times. He was on the phone to Chen last week."

"Wonderful," Tony said.

"And Chen had two calls from Robertson's personal cell phone last week."

"Is that all of it?"

"Clemens is flying in tomorrow," Joan said. "I've got his flight info right here. And a recent photo." She passed him the file folder.

Tony shuffled through the papers. "This is more than I expected. Thanks."

He turned to Missy. "You ready?"

Missy stood up and tucked in her shirt. "Thanks, Joan."

Tony turned back to Joan. He used a casual tone of voice. "Your daughter just showed up out of the blue. We never met."

"Of course."

Tony and Missy drove out to the Travel Ace truck stop at the freeway interchange for an early lunch. Truckers crowded the counter, and families from the nearby discount motels filled the tables. They sat in a booth against the back wall where they had a good view of the door and front windows. Tony ordered the breakfast special: two eggs, hash browns, toast, and bacon. Missy ordered yogurt and granola. The waitress brought their orders before Tony had a chance to finish his coffee.

"You going to make me watch you eat that?" Tony asked.

"I could say the same thing," Missy replied.

"Thanks for the assist back there."

"No problem. Joan really didn't understand what she'd gotten herself into."

"No, she didn't. I forgot to ask you how you know her."

"You think she'll make trouble when her daughter runs off? Call the cops?"

"The thought had crossed my mind."

"I met her through a girlfriend."

"Like the one you got now?"

"What can I say? I like civilians who think it's sexy to be with a player."

"And?"

"My girlfriend was a do-gooder. Volunteered at the women's shelter. Joan was hiding from her ex. A real peach. Put her in the hospital."

"Tell me if I'm wrong: Your girlfriend cried on your shoulder about the troubles of the world. You wanted to impress her, so you sent some guys to rob and murder him."

She smiled. "It got out of hand, but it couldn't have happened to a nicer fella. Don't know what happened to that girlfriend, but Joan has always been a friend."

"A friend who's good with computers."

"Yeah."

Tony pushed his plate away. "Sounds like she'll hold up."

"She always has."

"So Chen, Robertson, and Clemens were all in contact with one another," Tony said.

"Whatever that means," Missy said. "Robertson didn't try to kill you or arrest you."

"Maybe you're right and he's not a problem, or maybe he had to protect his cover. Maybe he double-crossed Chen, or maybe he's the luckiest guy in the world and just happened to be there to collect the info. Either way, I've still got business with the other players."

"What are you planning to do?"

"I'm going to meet Clemens at the airport and find out what he knows. Then I'll have a better idea of how to deal with the assholes who murdered my guys."

"Sure that's the best move? He might not know anything. He might be the next murder target."

"Chen's gone, Robertson's a Fed, so Clemens is the only move. Of course, you don't have to go with me. I've already told you that you can get off this merry-go-round whenever you like."

"Hey, I'm still in. I'm not going home until I'm sure I won't be bushwhacked."

"Then let's stay on course."

The server dropped a check on their table and collected their dishes.

They stood up. "I've got to see a guy about some gear," Tony said. "And he's kind of skittish, so I need to drop you somewhere."

"How long?"

"Maybe an hour. He's expecting me."

TONY DROVE through the gate to Sunny Days Recyclables, navigated through the mountains of scrap metal being sorted by huge cranes, and parked by the loading dock to a warehouse. A skinny guy with a shaved head wearing gray coveralls with the name *Barney* embroidered on the chest stood at the door. "He's expecting me," Tony said.

The guy led him into the warehouse, past crates stacked on pallets, to an office in the back. A short fat man who looked like an accountant or an insurance salesman stood up from his desk. "Trav. Great to see you."

"Thanks for helping me on such short notice."

"Need anything beside the Kevlar?"

"Two semiauto rifles, short barrels, and a clean vehicle."

"That makes us even."

They shook hands.

"Barney will fix you up."

They walked away from the office. "Follow me," Barney said. He led him through the warehouse to a pallet of boxes against the far wall. He slid out two cases. Inside each was an AR-15 rifle, a Glock 9mm, boxes of ammunition, and a Kevlar vest.

"Do these work for you?"

"They clean?" Tony asked.

"No serial numbers. They work fine."

"Great."

"What kind of ride do you need? Fast? Sporty?"

"Inconspicuous for city driving. Able to take a hit."

"I got you covered."

He pulled out a walkie-talkie. "Dennis, pull the Volvo up to the loading dock."

They carried the cases back through the warehouse to the loading dock. A yellow Volvo sedan sat parked next to the Corolla Tony had driven into the scrap yard. "Will that do?"

"Yeah."

"Yours hot?"

"Can you take care of it?"

"No problem."

They loaded the cases into the trunk of the Volvo. Tony climbed into the driver's seat.

MEANWHILE, Missy stood on the steps in front of the Mitchellville Public Library talking on her phone. A mom holding the hands of two preschoolers walked by. "That's right. The safecracker is going for Clemens at the airport."

"I told you to stay out of the way," Robertson said.

"I'm not sure if I can trust your partners. And you've been holding out on me. You didn't tell me Chen was dead."

"I feel sick about that. I tried to help him, but he wouldn't help himself."

"Well, my guy always has a way of landing on his feet."

"So I have to prove myself to you?"

"You don't have to prove anything. Either your partners are incompetent, or they're not listening to you. Either way is bad for me."

"You don't want to get in the middle of this business. You're part of my team. I can protect you. I did everything I could for Jerry, but he wouldn't listen to reason. The safecracker's guys, I'm sorry about that. That was overzealous bullshit. But if he doesn't let this thing go, he's going to get a bullet."

"He thinks your guys are hunting him, that they still want the envelope or want him dead. And he's sentimental about his partners."

"Nobody's hunting anyone. These bodies are just attracting the police."

"So I'm completely safe?"

"Completely safe."

The line was quiet.

"You there?" she asked.

"Do you want to make another five grand?"

"How?"

"Keep track of your guy so we can stay out of his way."

"Not set us both up to be killed?"

"This project is supposed to be accomplished without the knowledge of domestic law enforcement. How do you think that's been working so far? Two more days, that's all I need."

"Okay, I'll keep you up to speed. But at the first sign of trouble, I'm bolting."

She ended the call. Robertson had always been a handy person to know. He'd gotten her out of some jams, didn't ask for too much, but he wasn't her friend, not by a long shot. He sounded like he was telling the truth when he said she was safe, but that didn't mean she was safe, it just meant he thought she was. So how much work should she actually do for the extra five K? Tony wasn't her friend either, but he never turned on a partner, and he always got even. Narcing on him to Robertson would be like building her own gallows. So she had to walk a fine line—a thread, really. Give Robertson just enough so that he would believe she was on his side, and don't give up so much that Tony would see it as a definite betrayal. One of them was going to come out on top, and she planned to be standing next to whoever that was.

She called Betty. The phone rolled over to voice mail. "Hey, baby, just wanted to check on you. I'll try back later." She ended the call. Her phone rang. "Hey, lover."

Betty's voice sounded sleepy. "What time is it?"

"Eleven thirty. When did you go to bed?"

"You know I'm no good before noon. Where are you?"

"I'm at the library."

"Really?"

"Yeah. We're in the middle of things."

"Who's *we*?"

"A guy I know."

"He get you into this mess?"

"We got each other into it. How's your brother?"

"He's fine. His wife still hates me."

"Smile. Play nice."

"When can I go home?"

"Maybe in a few more days."

"A few more days?"

"I know it's a drag. As soon as it's safe, I'll let you know. I've got to go."

"Love you."

She sat down on a bench by the bus stop. Betty was such a prima donna. She couldn't think of a single reason why she loved her—and yet, just talking to her on the phone made her smile. This business of being on the run was so tedious. What had Robertson said? Two more days tops. She could juggle Robertson and Tony that long. Then she'd be back to sleeping with Betty and looking for her next score.

A half hour later, Tony pulled up in a Volvo sedan.

Missy climbed in. "I didn't know you were a family man. Get everything taken care of?"

"Yeah. I got Kevlar and AR-15s."

"Expecting to fight a war?"

"I'm not going to underestimate the scope of the problem. My guys were executed by professionals. If they come for me, they'll have their work cut out for them."

AT 2:00 P.M., Robertson and French stood on the sidewalk under a shade tree near the carousel in Fredrick Memorial Park. "Ring Around the Rosie" sounded from the carousel as the brightly painted animal figures went up and down and around in a circle. A bus marked Namaste Preschool idled at the curb. Several young women dressed in yoga wear stood in a group watching over a crowd of small children as they ran about on the grass, tumbling, jumping, and playing tag.

"So you did come down," French said. "Wasn't sure you'd really do it." Tobias French was an NGO contractor who used to be an army major. He had a way of speaking that made everything he said sound like he was giving an order.

"How was your flight?" Robertson asked.

"Sucked," French said. "Jet lag kills me anymore. Did you get the envelope?"

"Yeah. No thanks to your guys. They were in too big a hurry. I had to wait around for the safecracker with the bodies in the house."

"Did you deal with him?"

"Are you kidding? Out on the street in a suburban neighborhood?"

"But we've got the account info, and Chen's out of the way."

Robertson watched a man in a cable company uniform climb a utility pole on the corner.

"Don't worry about that guy. He's one of mine."

"The bank-account info is encrypted."

"So we still need Clemens."

"Yeah, and the safecracker's nosing around because we killed his partners."

"How do you know?"

"I've got a CI next to him. He's planning to take Clemens at the airport to find out what he knows."

"Then he's going to get cleaned up."

"But not my CI. She belongs to me. I promised her I'd look after her."

"She leads the lamb to the slaughter, we'll keep her safe."

"She'll take care of it. What about Clemens?"

"We'll meet him at the airport. He'll deal with the encryption, and we'll drop him somewhere where he won't be found."

"We've been over this. Dead criminals is one thing, but the Chens were already a step too far. His wife, for Christ's sake. And what your guys did to Jerry—he was a friend of mine."

"A friend who was going to screw you. Whose side are you on?"

"I'm just saying we can't have any more bodies. Particularly government employees."

"Paul, Clemens knows both of us. He's connected to Chen. There's something about him that's not right. You know it. I know it. Somebody alerted Kyrgyzstani Intelligence. You want to go to prison, or do you want the deluxe retirement package? My guys don't know any of the details; they're strictly muscle. As soon as Clemens is gone, I've got the back end, you've got the front end, and we're on our way to the money."

"The police are all over the Chens. They can't find any more crime scenes."

"You've got my word. Nobody will find him."

Robertson walked away. Where was it going to end? When French had told him they'd killed some of their Kyrgyzstani partners, he'd shrugged. Why should he care? Then when French had said Chen had to go, he had heard him say it, but he hadn't really believed he'd do it. Not here, not in the US. But Chen and Muriel, in their house—Jesus, what a mess. And the safecracker's crew. What was that about? That didn't have any logical purpose. Now French had his eye on Clemens. French had always been tightly wound, unwilling to let anything go, but now? It was a good thing they went so far back together. French couldn't have any doubts about him. As soon as they had the bank codes decrypted, they'd be able make the run for the money, and all this insanity would be behind him.

AT 4:00 P.M., Tony and Missy were in a room at the Budget More Motel on the access road off Jefferson Drive. Two beds with well-worn comforters, a square table with two chairs, a microwave sitting on top of a minifridge. The carpet had stains that were probably wine. A check on the internet showed that Clemens had made his flight, so barring any travel delays, he would be arriving on time tomorrow. There was a knock at the door. Tony looked through the peephole while Missy peered through a gap in the window curtain. A full-figured Latina in a black pantsuit stood at the door. She carried a shoulder bag, and a pistol was holstered on her hip. Tony opened the door.

"Yeah?"

The woman held up her ID. Clara Garcia, National Defense Agency.

"How did you find me?"

She rolled her eyes. "Please. Wasn't even a challenge. Can I come in?"

Tony backed into the room. Garcia nodded toward Missy before she shut the door behind herself.

"Why are you here?" Tony asked.

"You cracked Clemens's safe. Your guys were left at the Sundowner."

"I don't know what you're talking about."

"I've got video of you and your guy in Clemens's apartment. Looks like you killed your partners, killed the Chens, and kept all the loot for yourself."

"That's just BS."

"You're made for this. Murder squad won't look any farther."

"What if I tell them that your guy was at Chen's and he has the envelope from Clemens's safe?"

"When they quit laughing? Nobody will listen to you."

"What do you want?"

"You're going to get that envelope back."

"Talk to your associate."

"You want to be on my good side when the cavalry rolls in? Some folks are going to get clean away, and others are going for an extended stay at a black site."

"I could say yes and then run."

"Let me show you how I help my friends." Garcia pulled her laptop from her shoulder bag, opened it on the table, and put in a password. "What does this look like to you?"

Tony studied the screen. It was an FBI database.

"I can put stuff in, and I can take stuff out."

"Bullshit."

She inputted a case file number. Tony looked at the page. Gun running into Mexico. The Crazy Devils motorcycle gang. He and Nicole had made some good money on that scam.

"What do you think happens if I mark this case complete? The principal is in supermax; his lieutenants are lifers. You and your woman are the only ones left to be got."

"I don't believe you."

"What have you got to lose? You help me out, I'll help you out." She put away her laptop and set a cell phone on the table. "Here's a burner. Keep me in the loop."

Garcia left. Missy pulled back the curtain and watched her get into a Ford with a federal license plate. "Think she was real?"

"She acted real enough. And since she wants me to get the envelope, she must think the other guy is dirty. She wouldn't be making me an offer if she wasn't afraid she had a leak."

"Should we change motels?"

"No, changing motels would just make her think we're stupid."

"You going to help her?"

"I'm going to find a way to use her. If that involves helping her, yeah, I'll help her," Tony said.

"So our plan stays the same?"

"Clemens is still the key."

"If we're staying here, I'm going to the Quick Stop. Want anything?" Missy asked.

"Get some beer. I don't care what kind. And don't go to the Quick Stop on the corner. You'll want some room in case you pick up a tail."

"How would the bad guys find us?"

He handed her the car keys. "Got to assume they know where to look."

She got on the interstate and drove down two exits before she got off on Chandler Trail. There was a Stop-N-Go on the corner. She pulled in and parked facing out. Before she went into the store, she called Robertson. "Hey, it's me. One of your people showed up. She wants help getting the envelope back."

"Who?"

"Garcia."

"I know who you're talking about. Did you share any info with her?"

"No."

"Did she show her hand?"

"No, she just spun out a hypothetical to try to scare my guy."

"Did it work?"

"My guy doesn't scare."

"With Garcia in the mix, I need to do some homework. What's the safecracker's name?"

"I'm not telling you that. You start snooping, he finds out, I'm dead."

"You think I'm that stupid?"

"I think your friends don't give a shit."

"He still planning on snatching Clemens?"

"Yep."

"Do whatever you have to do to stay out of the way tomorrow."

LATER, in the motel room, while Missy was in the bathroom getting ready for bed, Tony sat at the table watching the door to the bathroom. There was something about her that made him uneasy, something he just couldn't put his finger on. Missy had been very helpful so far. Almost too helpful. Coming in with him. Offering Joan. The drive-by at the drug house. Agreeing to the airport plan. She didn't even bail after Garcia had turned up. Why? She should have been arguing about something. Sure, she probably was really afraid of being murdered by the bad guys. Maybe she was even afraid for her girlfriend. But that just didn't seem like enough to keep her in this game. What did she know that she wasn't sharing? If Nicole were here, they would have cut Missy loose as soon as they had known she wasn't responsible for Duke's and Barker's murders. But Nicole wasn't here, and he needed a partner. But not a partner who'd betray him.

Missy had claimed she was just the go-between, that all she'd done was put him and Chen together. And maybe that was true. Or maybe she'd followed Duke and Barker from the job. Had some guys ready to go. Planned to hijack the diamonds but didn't find them. All the rest of it could be exactly the same: bad guys murdering the Chens, hunting the supposed blackmail envelope, Clemens being their only lead. But if that was the real story, why hadn't she tried to take the diamonds and the cash? She knew he had them. She didn't know the diamonds were in the PO box. Was she just hoping to make sure he was dead before she made her play? Was she that afraid he'd come after her? He heard the toilet flush.

If he needed to kill her, now would be better than later. She wasn't going to be much use tomorrow. Running and gunning and kidnapping weren't in her wheelhouse. But she could drive, and she had plenty of local connections. So maybe she could still be useful. Besides, he didn't want to kill her if she wasn't a bad player. Bodies drew cops like picnics drew ants.

When Missy came out of the bathroom wearing men's pajamas, Tony heard Nicole's voice in his head: *You know you can't trust her.*

"What are you looking at?" Missy asked.

Tony smiled. He needed to keep her off her guard. "You really do prefer men's clothes."

"You think I'm going to get all sexy for you?"

"Not trying to go there," Tony said.

"I know all about you and your woman. You'll sleep with anyone to cement a con."

"And you won't?"

"I've got standards."

"You only lie to beautiful women."

"I only *sleep* with beautiful women," Missy said.

"And your girl Betty? Is she window dressing or true love?"

"Why you asking?"

"Seems like a fair question to me."

"She's none of your business. She's not in the game."

"Okay."

"I'm not kidding."

"I hear you." He nodded toward the bathroom. "You done

in there?"

"Yeah."

Tony went into the bathroom. Loyal to her girl. Maybe he could use that to his advantage. And she was afraid he'd find a way to manipulate her. He closed the door and turned on the faucet. Or maybe she didn't give a shit about Betty. Maybe this show of sentimentality was her way of trying to manipulate him. There were always multiple interpretations of any behavior. Bottom line, he'd never be able to trust her, but that didn't mean he couldn't use her. At least for now. He just needed to take precautions in case she planned to sell him out.

BACK IN THE San Francisco Bay Area, it was Ladies Night at Lucky Joe's. Lily had found out about this place from an old boyfriend. It was located in a rundown neighborhood not all that far by car from the regentrifying zone where she lived, and it was safe for women on their own. Lily was standing with two men at the bar. The music was loud. Country top forty. She'd come in for a drink when she'd noticed these guys in the back. They were business guys, middle-aged, they'd lost their neckties somewhere, and they didn't belong here among the construction workers and the Walmart checkers. So she'd sashayed back to flirt some free drinks. The younger one, a pudgy guy with a shaved head and a sad mustache, was the talker. The other one, tall and thin with a bad comb-over, seemed to be his boss. As she sipped her martini, batted her eyes, brushed against them, made her small talk, she became bored. These guys were looking for hookers, and that wasn't her. She kept thinking about the wedding reception, taking the Porsche convertible, driving down the boulevard. Nicole had been there, but she'd lifted the keys herself. It was surprisingly easy to do. Could she do it again?

She lurched into Shaved Head, ran her hands up and down the front of his jacket as if she were trying to get her balance, slipped her hand into his jacket pocket, and palmed his car key fob. "Whoa," she said. "Did you see that guy bump into me?" She picked up her martini and took a drink. "Don't run away, guys. I'm going to the ladies'."

She squeezed through a knot of dancers in front of the band—cowboy hats and lizard-skin boots—glanced over her shoulder to make sure Shaved Head and Comb-over weren't watching her, scooted past the women's restroom, and pushed through the back door into the parking lot. What was he driving? She squinted at the fob. BMW. She pressed the Unlock button as she walked. The tail-lights flashed on a blue BMW sedan.

Just then, the back door slammed behind her. "Stop!"

Shaved Head was running toward her, Comb-over sauntering after him with his hands in his pockets and a bemused look on his face.

She put one hand on the trunk of the BMW and cocked her head as if she were drunk. "What's up?"

"You stole my car keys."

"Car keys?" She glanced around as if she expected them to be lying on the pavement instead of in her hand.

He grabbed her wrist and snatched the fob from her. "You little bitch."

She tried to move away, but he jerked her around, smacked her, and pushed her into Comb-over's arms.

"I'll scream."

"Shut up." He dug through her purse until he found her driver's license. "Lily Crockett." He tossed the purse onto the trunk of the car. "Well, Lily, you can work this off, or you can go to jail."

Everything was happening in slow motion. She looked from one to the other, their leering grins and glassy eyes. She was trapped between the cars. Her lip tasted of blood. She wasn't going to let them fuck her. And she couldn't get arrested. She tried to push past Comb-over, but Shaved Head grabbed her by the shoulders and spun her around against the car.

"Let go of me."

"You can quit pretending. We've seen all the tricks you little whores play."

She kicked him in the shin. He gripped her forearms and forced his knee between her legs. His breath smelled of whiskey and bar food.

A woman yelled, "Let her go!"

Lily turned. A man and a woman were coming across the parking lot, the woman in front, yelling and pointing. The man was digging his phone from his pocket.

Shaved Head pushed her away. He yelled at Comb-over, "Let's go!"

Lily stumbled to the far end of the parking stall.

Shaved Head grabbed her purse off the trunk. He and Comb-over jumped into the BMW and screeched out of the lot.

Lily was sitting on the asphalt. Her heart was pounding. She was gasping for air. The woman knelt down beside her. "Are you okay, sugar?"

"My bag. Do you see my bag?"

The man shook his head.

The woman rubbed Lily's back. "Do you want us to call the police? Do you need help?"

Lily crawled up the fender of the car in the next stall. "No. I'm okay."

"You sure? Those guys belong in jail. We saw the whole thing."

"No, I'm okay." Lily started walking away.

"Do you need a ride? Our car is right here. Let us help you."

"I THOUGHT you'd be home by now." Martha Robertson's voice on the phone had a hard edge.

"Me too," Robertson said. He was sitting up, fully clothed, on the bed in a hotel room in Mitchellville. The side table lamp was on, creating a pool of light in the otherwise dark room.

"Where are you anyway?"

"You know I can't tell you that. How were the mountains? Did Meagan go with you?"

"She did. The quilt show was amazing—lots of beautiful patterns.

One quilt was like the one your mother keeps in the spare bedroom. The bluegrass was what you'd expect. A few great pickers and a lot of enthusiasm. And we went horseback riding on some forest trails. Not my thing, as you well know, but Meagan wanted to go. It wasn't too bad. I didn't fall off."

"Sounds like you had a good time."

"A great time. Most of the food was mediocre, but that French restaurant you googled ahead of time was fabulous."

"I'm glad. Wish I could have been there. I'm hoping to get home in a couple more days."

"I'm not holding my breath."

"I didn't do this on purpose. I go where they send me."

"Craig called. He was surprised you weren't with me."

"That's the kind of job this is, which is why I really can't say anything about it. Just repeat after me: 'Six months until full pension; six months until full pension.'"

"Good night, dear." She ended the call.

Robertson turned on the TV. He should have been with her in the mountains. He'd never get out of couples' counseling at this rate. If he could only tell her what he was up to, that he was securing their retirement, that he was doing this for her. But that was impossible now. Goddamn French and his paranoia. There hadn't been any reason to kill anybody. If French had followed the plan to begin with, he wouldn't have scared the hell out of Chen. But no, he was sure their Kyrgyzstani partners were dirty, so they had to go. Then Chen had to wet his pants. Now Chen was dead, and Clemens was going to die. And he was going to have to make sure that the local cops and the FBI never figured out who had committed the murders. He was beginning to wonder whether the money was worth the risk.

MEANWHILE, in San Francisco, Nicole wandered into the den in her pajamas, her robe fluttering behind her. Denison was sitting at one end of the sofa, reading something on his iPad. "There you are," she said. "Wasn't Bell supposed to call today?"

"Yeah. Don't know how I forgot to tell you. She's having trouble finding a wedding venue."

"I thought she was going to keep things simple," Nicole said.

"It's not like here. There aren't that many places within driving range, and she's been so busy teaching this semester that she started late."

"And now it's hard to find a place for the date she wants."

"Exactly."

"Do you want anything in particular for the wedding?" Nicole said.

"No. That's something Stacey would have had definite opinions about. I just want Bell to be happy."

"What would Stacey have wanted?"

"She liked a formal wedding. Fancy dress, women wearing hats, wedding held on the bride's home turf. You should have seen Skip's."

"So she'd be orchestrating the whole thing if she were still alive."

"She'd be driving Bell crazy. But since she's not here—"

"Bell is missing her mom."

"And I'm a poor substitute."

"But you're Stacey's proxy."

"Yeah."

"So you've got to keep on acting like you care about the details and you think she's making good decisions."

"I'll just be glad when it's all over."

The doorbell rang. They both went to the front door. Lily stood on the stoop, her high heels in one hand. Her dress was torn. Her hair was disheveled, and her makeup was smeared. Tears ran down her cheeks.

"Lily," Nicole said.

"This is Lily?" Denison asked.

"I couldn't go home," Lily said.

"Come in," Nicole said. She put her arm around her. A car that had been idling at the curb drove away. Nicole glanced up and down the street before she closed the door.

"Who attacked you?" Nicole asked.

"He got my bag. Some people gave me a ride."

She led Lily into the den. "Sit down."

Denison went to the side table and poured Lily a glass of whiskey. She sat on the sofa holding the glass with both hands.

"Where were you at?" Nicole asked.

"I was in this bar. Out in the parking lot, these guys jumped me. Some people helped me, brought me here."

"Start at the beginning."

Lily glanced from Nicole to Denison and back.

Nicole sat down beside her. "It's okay. You can talk in front of James."

"I was out messing around."

"By yourself?"

She nodded. "I went into Lucky Joe's. It's fun there sometimes. Some business dudes were in there. Never seen them before."

"So you went to work on them."

"They caught me in the parking lot with their car keys."

"Jesus," Denison said.

"You should never do something like that on your own," Nicole continued.

"I know that now."

"So they smacked you around?"

"I've never been so scared. They were going to fuck me for trying to take the car. I didn't want them to beat me. Or call the cops. But then a couple came out of the bar. The woman screamed."

"And they brought you here?"

"Yeah, but my handbag is gone. I think those guys have it—my driver's license, credit cards, the works."

"You think they're going to your apartment?"

"I don't know. I'm afraid to go there. And my other friends. . ." She looked at her lap.

"You're staying here tonight," Denison said. He pointed at Nicole. "And you're not going over there."

"Not tonight," she said.

"Am I the only grown-up in the room? You should call the cops."

"No cops," Lily said.

Nicole looked at Denison. "We don't need to get into this now. I'm going to put Lily in Bell's room."

She took Lily by the hand and led her down the hall and up the stairs.

"I wouldn't have come here if I had any place else to go," Lily said.

"Don't worry about it."

"James seemed a little pissed off."

"It'll be okay. How drunk were those guys?"

"Pretty drunk, but they weren't slurring. They were slumming it, looking for prostitutes."

"But they were going to rape you in the parking lot?"

"They weren't calling it that. They thought I was a prostitute, that I'd trade sex for silence. If that couple hadn't come out of the bar—"

"So they were going to bully you into the sex?"

"Sex or they call the cops. What should I do now? I need to get my bag back."

"You're safe now. Sleep on it. You can't do anything until tomorrow anyway."

She turned on the lights as they entered Bell's bedroom. "The bathroom is stocked. And Bell keeps some clothes here, so there's probably some jammies in the dresser."

"You're a life saver." Lily hugged her.

"Don't worry about it." She rubbed Lily's back. "We'll get this sorted out tomorrow."

Nicole went back downstairs to the den. Denison was standing at the windows looking out onto the street. "She going to be all right?"

"Yeah. I'm sorry about all this." She tried to take his hand, but he pulled away.

"I didn't realize what you meant when you said you'd been flirting for drinks. This is crazy risky."

"It is if you don't know what you're doing."

"What are you going to do now?"

"Help Lily if she needs it. I told you no more secrets. I won't do any more baby scams. Not one free drink. Not one stolen car."

"Seriously?"

"Really."

SANDERS TURNED into the parking deck next to ACS Associates in a nearby suburb and drove up two levels to Kirby's Audi. The deck was empty, except for three cars that probably belonged to the building security team. He pulled in beside the Audi and put the BMW in park. "We've got to get our story straight."

Kirby laughed. "That was crazy."

Sanders ran his hand over his moustache. "There're probably security cameras in the parking lot."

Kirby's face fell. "You think the cops will be after us?"

"If that couple got my license plate number and called the police."

"I can't have this."

"Me neither. Okay. The woman picked my pocket."

"She did."

"We caught her trying to steal my car."

"Also true."

"We tussled. The couple started yelling. We ran because we're drunk, didn't want the cops involved, didn't want the publicity, were afraid we'd be arrested."

"That's our story?"

"That's it."

"Okay. That'll be easy to remember." Kirby was quiet for a moment. "What about the girl?"

"What about her?"

"You took her handbag."

Sanders looked into the back seat. The handbag was sitting in the floor. "I'll put the fear of God in her. Make sure she keeps quiet."

"Okay." Kirby opened the car door. He started chuckling. "The look on your face when you realized she had your car keys—I'm never going to forget that. How bad are you going to mess with her?"

"She tried to steal my car, almost got us arrested. She deserves a little trouble."

5

THE AIRPORT PICKUP

Wednesday morning, Tony squinted at his watch in the dark. It was 5:15 a.m. He glanced at Missy in the other bed. She was snoring softly. He gathered his clothes and went into the bathroom to get dressed. It was time to set up his getaway plan. He slipped out of the motel room with his go bag, took the beltway to the east side of Mitchellville, and got off at Sixty-third Street. On one side of the divided highway was a rundown Trucker's Delight truck stop. On the other side was WeekStay Motel, a strip of rooms with peeling paint and a potholed parking lot. He counted four cars parked in front of the rooms, none of them new. It was just the place he was looking for. He pulled into a spot in front of the office. The door was locked. He pressed the buzzer on the intercom. A voice said, "We open at seven."

"I need a room now," Tony said.

"Check in is at ten. You can wait in the truck stop across the way."

"I'll pay for the week in cash. Starting yesterday."

The lights in the office came on. A middle-aged woman in a heavy robe and furry slippers came to the door. The butt of a pistol hung out of her robe pocket. She studied Tony for a moment before turning the lock. She shuffled off behind the counter while Tony came in.

"The week?" she asked.

"Yesterday through next Wednesday."

"In cash?"

"Yeah."

"Five hundred dollars."

"That much?"

"Uh-huh."

He laid five one-hundred-dollar bills on the counter. She handed him a key. "Second from the end," she said.

He went down to the room and looked inside. Stained carpet, scratched furniture, thin towels. The faint smell of urine and disinfectant. The kind of place where nobody minded your business. He dropped the go bag on the bed, shifted the mattress, slashed the cover to the box spring, and put his Glock and the envelope containing the $5,000 down in the box spring. Then he shifted the mattress back and straightened the bedspread. He put the Do Not Disturb sign on the doorknob as he left.

On his way back to the Budget More Motel, he noticed a line of cars at a Dunkin' Donuts drive-through and pulled in. He bought an assortment of donuts, a large coffee, and a large tea. He cradled the cup carrier of drinks and the bag of donuts in one arm as he opened the motel room door. Missy raised her head up from her pillow when the outside light slanted into the room.

She squinted at him, her pistol in her hand. "Where you been?"

"Went out for breakfast. Brought you some tea." He set the bag of donuts and the cup carrier on the table.

She sat up on the edge of her bed and set her pistol on the night table. "Thanks."

"Can I turn on the light?"

"Go ahead."

"You like anything in your tea?"

"Where's it from?"

"Dunkin' Donuts."

"One cream, one sugar."

He fixed her tea and carried it to her. Then he sat down at the table, took the cover off his coffee, and blew on it.

Missy looked at her smartphone. "Clemens is still on time. Plane landed in New York. He'll still be here at ten."

Tony tapped his donut on his napkin to knock the loose sprinkles off. "Excellent."

"What's the plan?"

"No hurry. We can talk after you're ready for the day."

"I'd rather talk now." She sipped her tea.

"We've got his picture, so he'll be easy enough to spot. I'm going to hold up a sign with his name on it. With any luck, he'll fall right into our hands. No muss, no fuss. Show him a gun if I need to."

"Bring him back here?"

"That depends. Is he a hard guy? Does he know what's going on? Or is he a chump? You know how I work. I want the least mess possible. Maybe we drop him at his apartment. Maybe we bring him here. Maybe we dump him in the country. It just depends on who he is and what we find out."

"Okay."

"In the meantime, since we're talking it through, I want to pick up a different car for the airport."

"You going to swap out the Volvo?"

"No, it's clean. You can drop me and bring it back here."

She got up with her tea in her hand and started toward the bathroom. "I'll be ready in a few minutes."

"Great. You want any of these donuts?"

"Save me one with chocolate icing."

Missy and Tony drove into downtown on the tail end of rush hour and took a left into a parking deck next to an office tower. Tony scanned the parked cars as they spiraled up through the parking deck. Partway up the third level, he said, "Stop. That black Lincoln is perfect."

"Wait for you?"

"No need."

Missy turned toward the exit as Tony was walking toward the Lincoln Navigator. She bounced over the speed bump at the gate and turned right headed for the beltway. Panhandlers were working the intersections. She fell in behind a school bus. It took a left, and she continued another block to the beltway ramp. The beltway traffic was mainly semitrucks and commercial vehicles, all moving fast. As she was driving north around town, her phone vibrated. It was Robertson.

"It's me," she said.

"Your guy still going to the airport?"

"Yeah."

"You really, really don't want to be there."

"Not my call."

"We're going to get Clemens ahead of you. Make sure you're the one driving when you start after us. Get lost in traffic. That's your best bet."

"What do you think my guy is going to do if he thinks I'm jerking him around? I agreed to provide you with information, not set myself up to be killed."

"I don't want anything to happen to you, but if you come after us and we get in a gunfight, I won't be able to protect you until the shooting stops. That's all I'm saying. Make your best choice."

When Missy got back to the motel room, she started wiping down the surfaces, beginning with the bathroom, and working methodically through the bedroom, being sure to include the TV remote and the lamp switches. It was unlikely that they would be trailed here by law enforcement, even more unlikely that there would be any reason to fingerprint the room, and they might be back here with Clemens in a few hours, but wiping down a room had always been strangely relaxing for her, and she didn't want nerves to give her away to Tony before the shooting started—if it was going to start. It wouldn't surprise her at all if Tony managed to steal Clemens out from under their noses, find some way to get one step ahead of them, but if it all turned to mud, she was going to make sure that she was the last person he blamed. While she was wiping off the minifridge, Tony came in.

"Where you been?"

"Drove around awhile. Wanted to make sure I wasn't being followed."

She turned back to the minifridge. There was something about his tone of voice, his manner, the way he moved—he was just a little too—calm? Certain? Something was up—something he wasn't sharing. That banter last night, his oh so obvious trust, the cup of tea this morning—was it all real, or was it a ploy to put her at ease, to keep her from seeing that she was about to be played? He was a master at getting inside a mark's head. She had to stay on her guard.

BACK IN SAN FRANCISCO, the sun was just slanting over the buildings across the street. Denison and Nicole were sitting at the kitchen island. He was reading the newspaper and sipping his coffee. An empty cereal bowl sat to his right. Nicole was reading the newspaper on her smartphone and eating granola mixed with yogurt. She glanced up. A jogger passed by on the sidewalk. The neighbors from across the street, business clothes and brief cases, got into their car. Lily came into the room in the wrinkled party dress she'd been wearing the night before.

"How did you sleep?" Nicole asked.

"Fine."

"There's coffee on the counter. Breakfast stuff."

"No thanks. Could you lend me cab fare? I need to go home and get ready for work."

Denison set his paper down. "Are you serious? What if those guys are waiting for you?"

"Those guys are at home nursing hangovers. My neighbor has a spare door key. It's six thirty in the morning. I'm perfectly safe."

"I've got some cash in my purse," Nicole said.

"Can I borrow your phone to call a cab?"

Nicole handed Lily her smartphone. "Yellow Cab is in the Contacts."

Lily called a cab and passed the smartphone back to Nicole.

"Come on," Nicole said. "I'll get you your money."

They walked into the front hall where Nicole's handbag hung on a coat-tree. She took out a wad of cash and pressed it into Lily's hand. "To help tide you over until you get your ID straightened out."

"Thanks. I'll pay you back."

"No hurry."

Nicole opened the door so that they could watch for the cab. "Have you decided how to handle those guys?"

"If I'm lucky, they'll feel stupid this morning and will be happy to give me back my bag."

"If not?"

"I haven't gotten that far."

"If you need help, just let me know."

"Thanks."

A cab pulled up in front of the condo. "There it is," Lily said.

"Call me later," Nicole said.

"I will."

Nicole walked back to the kitchen. Denison was rinsing the breakfast dishes in the sink. "Do you really think she's safe?"

Nicole shrugged. "I don't know."

AT THE MITCHELLVILLE AIRPORT at ten minutes to ten, Tony and Missy sat in the Lincoln Navigator at the far end of the drop-off lane where they had a good view of arrivals and departures. Travelers were rolling bags to and from the parking garage across to the terminal. The skycaps were busy with the passengers who wanted to avoid carrying their luggage inside. A light mist began to fall. Tony put the windshield wipers on intermittent. A white Mercedes sedan pulled into the drop-off lane in front of the main entrance. Three men got out: Robertson, a middle-aged guy with a gray crew cut, and a thick-necked guy in a leather coat.

"We're screwed," Tony said.

"What?" Missy peered about like she didn't know what Robertson looked like.

"Two o'clock. Robertson and two other guys. Management and muscle, looks like. They're going to collect Clemens."

The three men stood on the sidewalk waiting. Tony held a picture of Clemens. "There he is. Freckles and all."

A blond man wearing a gray suit came up to the three men, smiled, and shook hands with Robertson and Gray Crew Cut. Tony took their picture with his phone. They all piled into the Mercedes.

"I guess we're tailing them," Tony said.

"You sure that's a good idea? We don't want to go anywhere we can't get away from."

"They're our only lead."

Tony followed them out of the airport, cut around a minivan to stay with them, and fell into traffic a few cars behind. "I love an SUV for a surveillance job."

The mist turned to rain. The Mercedes headed away from downtown, took two rights onto a street lined with warehouses, and turned left into the entry of a Mighty Fortress Self Storage. A man in a raincoat and a ball cap shut the gate. Tony parked on the side of the street.

"Are we going to wait?" Missy asked.

"Can't find out what's going on from here. We already know Robertson and Clemens are connected. And we already know that Robertson has the blackmail envelope."

"They might not know anything about the people who killed your partners."

"True. But who is that other guy? We've seen him and two others who aren't cops. Are they the cleanup crew? Maybe their base is in there. Maybe we can learn something or get a chance to snatch Clemens."

"I already told you running and gunning is not my thing."

"You've done okay so far. This is just a simple little recon."

"I could stay in the car."

"I need you with me. Gear up."

They climbed into the back of the Navigator, opened the gun cases, and took out the Kevlar vests and the AR-15 rifles. Thunder cracked in the distance. The rain was bouncing off the sidewalk as they slipped through the gate, came around a dumpster, and moved along the side of a block of self-storage units. Ahead, on the left, they could see the Mercedes parked beside the rental office. The Mercedes was empty. Tony peeked in the nearest window of the office. He couldn't see anyone. They crept to the left corner of the building. No one was visible on the street. The rain slowed. They sneaked along the wall to the next window. Tony leaned over to peek in.

A shot chipped the concrete near Tony's foot, the gunshot almost on top of the bullet strike. The shooter was close, too close. Tony glanced over his shoulder while he scrambled backward. Missy was gone. Another shot. The window above him shattered. He crawled faster, the gunshots herding him back toward the corner of the building. Then a shot hit the wall behind him. He rolled out from the wall, sprang up, and zigzagged through the rain toward the nearest block of storage units, firing blindly as he ran. Automatic gunfire buzzed around him like hornets. He fell to the ground behind the side of the storage unit. His legs felt wobbly. He couldn't breathe. He thought he'd been hit in the vest. He sat with his back against the wall and his rifle across his knees. He forced himself to suck in air. *Don't pass out. Dead men pass out.*

His heart was pounding as he climbed to his feet. This place was a trap. He needed to keep moving. He could hear footsteps. Thunder sounded. Rain pounded the pavement. Someone tackled him. They rolled across the asphalt. A big guy, heavy, was on top of him, one hand pushing into his face. He jerked his head sideways. A knife struck the pavement next to his throat. He grabbed the wrist of the hand that held the knife. The man's face was inches from his. Cold eyes and hot breath. He clapped his other hand around the back of the man's head and bit down hard on his nose. The man jerked away, blood pouring down his face. Tony pulled his Glock, shot the man twice, sprang to his feet, and ran for the next corner. His head was spinning. He crawled under a pile of boxes by the door to a storage unit and tried to control his breathing. The rain poured down.

Later, when he woke, it was dark and quiet. His side hurt, and his tongue was stuck to the roof of his mouth. He tried to spit. Where was he? The events filtered back into his mind. He crawled out from under the boxes. Every movement hurt, but he got to his feet and stumbled back toward the rental office, both hands cradling the assault rifle. The Mercedes was gone. He leaned against a wall. His clothes were damp, but he felt wetness oozing from underneath his Kevlar vest. Had he been shot? He put his hands on his knees and breathed. Missy? Was she dead or going on his list? She hadn't wanted to come in here. Was that because she didn't know, or because she knew and didn't want him to get hurt, or because she knew and was afraid she'd be shot in the crossfire?

He made his way to the gate, stood next to the dumpster, and peered down the street. The Navigator was gone, and the street was empty. He pulled off the Kevlar, wiped it and the rifle as best he could with his handkerchief, and dropped them into the dumpster. The Glock he slipped into his waistband under his shirt. Then he looked at his side. Sure enough, he was trickling blood. He put his hand over the wound and pressed gently. He winced against the pain. *Not too bad.* He tried to stand up straight and walk naturally. His clothes were a mess, but the night sky was dark with clouds. *Got to keep moving.* He took a few tentative steps. This wasn't going to work. He leaned up against the chain-link fence and looked up a taxi company on his smartphone.

When the taxi pulled up, he got in the back, acting drunk, and slid down in the seat. "Where to?" the driver said.

He gave him the address of the Trucker's Delight truck stop.

"You get lost, brother?" the driver asked.

"Lost?"

"I never picked up a fare out here before."

"I've got an extra fifty that says your fare wasn't here."

"Let me see it."

Tony held up a wad of twenties.

The driver got on the radio. "There's nobody here. I'm headed back downtown."

When they got to the truck stop, Tony leaned against the outside wall away from the doors while he watched the taxi drive away. Then he hobbled across the divided highway, clutching his side, and made his way to his motel room. The Do Not Disturb sign was still on the door. He turned on the lights with the door open. No one was waiting for him. He shut the door, locked it, and stumbled across the room to the bathroom. He pulled up his bloody shirt. There was a hole in his lower outside abdomen oozing blood. It couldn't be too bad. He'd been shot hours ago, and he was still on his feet. He peeled off his dirty clothes, dropped them into the bathtub, and then grabbed a washcloth off the shelf over the toilet, ran it under the faucet, and wiped himself off. The wound was still seeping. He pressed a clean washcloth against it.

He found a roll of duct tape in the go bag he'd left on the bed. He pulled the end free with his teeth and wrapped the tape around his waist to secure the washcloth. What else had he brought? Change of clothes. His other gun and his money were in the box spring. He went back into the bathroom and drank a full glass of water. Then another. Thus far, he was doing okay, but he needed a doctor. This wound was going to get worse, not better. He put on clean underwear and crawled up on the bed. There was no one he trusted who could help him from here. Not anyone he would trust with his life. There could be a bullet in him. He could wake up with a fever and puss even if the bullet had gone straight through. If he went to the emergency room with a gunshot wound, he'd wind up in jail. He had no choice. He picked up his phone and made the call.

"Hello?" Nicole sounded as if he'd woken her.

"I fucked up," he said.

"Are you safe?"

"Yeah. I got shot. I'm okay, but I need your help."

"You still in Mitchellville?"

"Yeah."

"What's your address?"

He told her.

"It's going to take me most of twenty-four hours to get there. Should I reach out?"

"No, I've got trust issues right now. I'm not leaking too much. I just can't manage on my own."

"You sure?"

"Yeah."

"I'm on my way."

"I'll be here."

NICOLE CLIMBED out of bed in the dark. "What's up?" Denison asked.

"Tony needs my help."

He rolled toward her. "What? Right now? It's the middle of the night."

"Go back to sleep. I have to make some preparations. We'll talk in the morning. I promise."

She slipped on her robe as she walked down the hall to the living room. What had Tony gotten himself into? These simple little pass-the-time jobs were going to be the death of him. He was shot, reaching out to her, so Duke and the other guy must be dead or in the wind. She poured herself a glass of water. But he wasn't hurt badly enough to take a chance on a friend of a friend. He was willing to wait for her. She needed to line up a doctor and a full set of heavy gear. She speed-dialed Billy.

He was wide-awake. "What's up, Missus? Haven't heard from you in a while."

"I need a combat package."

"How many?"

"Two, one with a sniper setup," she said.

"Where you fighting this war?"

"Mitchellville."

"Where your old man is? You can have it tomorrow."

"And I need a doc."

"I don't have a doc in Mitchellville. Can you drive?"

"Rather not."

"I've got a vet."

"That'll have to do."

"Okay, hang on a second while I look this up." The line was quiet. "Got a pencil?"

"Go."

"Danny Newberry at Happy Pets Clinic. 1145 Washington Trail."

"Got you."

"He'll be expecting you. And my guy will be in contact with you to set up the drop—probably one o'clock at the earliest."

"I'll be traveling tomorrow, so I may have to return his call."

"No problem."

"Thanks, Billy. Send a bill through the usual account, and I'll transfer the cash."

"Good luck."

She got out her laptop computer and looked at possible airplane reservations. Three airlines. No direct flight into Mitchellville. But Washington, DC? One first-class ticket left into BWI Marshall Airport. Eight a.m. She bought it. Then she went back into the bedroom and slipped into bed.

Denison pulled her close. "Did you get it sorted out?"

His beard brushed against her cheek, and she breathed in his scent. "We're not talking about it tonight, Jimmy. Everything is okay. I've got my plan in place. We'll talk about it in the morning."

"I'm awake now."

"I know." She ran her hand down his arm and let it rest at his waist. She kissed him. "I love you."

"I won't be able to sleep until you tell me."

She sighed. "You really want to know right now?"

"I have to know."

"Okay." She filled in the details.

"That's everything?"

"Uh-huh."

"Tony could be dead before you get there. Killers could be waiting for you."

"I'm leaving here at six fifteen. I'll be gone three days to a week."

"This is crazy."

"I'll call you every day."

"Do you think that makes it better?"

"And I need for you to help Lily if she needs anything."

"Super."

"It's just until I get back."

"What if those guys come here?"

"Why would they do that?"

"But what if they break in?"

"Run. Call the cops."

"You're making me crazy."

She kissed him again. "Enough. It's time to sleep." She rolled over and backed up against him. "Hold me." He put his arms around her. She folded her arms across her chest and held his forearms. "That's better. Go to sleep."

6

CHANGING THE GAME

Nicole and Denison sat at the kitchen island. Denison was still in his robe, while Nicole was dressed in a black pantsuit. Her hair was pulled back at the nape of her neck. She took a sip of coffee. "Any more questions?"

"You shouldn't go."

"Jimmy, we've been over this."

"It's too dangerous."

"Jimmy, when I came back, I didn't lie to you. I told you that I was going to help Tony whenever he needed me. That's the way it has to be."

"I know. I just didn't—"

"You were hoping he'd never call."

"I didn't realize what it would feel like."

She reached across the island and took his hand. "I love you. And if you change your mind, if you don't want me anymore, that will be hard. I'd be sorry a long time. But the reason I wasn't afraid going after Bell was because I knew if things went bad he'd be coming after me. No doubt. No questions. When he calls, I'm going to go."

"And you aren't afraid?"

"Of course I'm afraid. God knows what I'm going to find. I'm just going to make myself ready for whatever comes."

"Well, I don't care about him. I'm in love with you."

"And I love you. Everything about you. But I'm going to go help him." She looked out the window. "The cab is here."

He followed her into the front hall. Her suitcase was by the door. She kissed him. He held her, his eyes closed, imprinting the feel of her body in his mind.

"I'll be back before you know it."

"I hope so."

She put on a pair of fake glasses, opened the door, and waved at the taxi. "I'll call when I land."

MIDMORNING, Lily sat at her desk at Travel Dreams travel agency looking at her desk phone. She needed to get her handbag back. Her wallet, her driver's license, her credit cards, and her phone were in it. It was a mistake carrying her life around with her when she was flirting up strangers. She should have just had cash in her pocket. She knew that now. And she knew what she had to do. It was simple. Call her phone. Talk to whoever answered. Get them to agree to give up her stuff. Meet in daylight in public. But yesterday, she just hadn't been able to bring herself to do it. Whenever she'd picked up a phone to input her smartphone number, she had felt that guy's hands on her shoulders, smelled his breath in her face. She'd been such an idiot. She could, of course, cancel the credit cards, replace the phone, report the driver's license as stolen, but those guys knew her name and her address. She had to know if she was safe. She couldn't put it off any longer. She picked up the desk phone and input her phone number.

Her smartphone rang and rang, but no one answered. The call moved over to voice mail. No help there. Without the phone password, they couldn't see the voice mail. She hung up. Had they thrown her bag in a dumpster that night or the next morning? Had she been worried about her personal safety all this time for no reason?

Her desk phone rang. She was startled. *Crazy thinking. It can't be them.* She put her hand on her chest and took a deep breath before she picked it up. "Travel Dreams. We make your dreams come true. How can I help?"

"Chrissie, please."

She transferred the call. She was just winding herself up. Making herself even more anxious. She needed to settle down. Maybe they just couldn't get to her phone in time. She called herself again. The phone rang. She was about to hang up when someone answered.

"Hello," a man's voice said.

She glanced around to make sure no one was in listening range. "You took my handbag."

"You tried to steal my car."

"I want my bag back."

He chuckled. "With the phone and the wallet?"

"Yes."

"What have you got to trade?"

"To trade?"

"I got this bag, and its contents, fair and square. If you want it back, you're going to have to give me something in return."

"Like what?"

"I'm sure you'll think of something. And remember, Lily, I know your name, where you work, and where you live, so don't do anything stupid."

"Are you threatening me?"

"Call me back when you've decided what you want to trade."

The line went dead. Vomit started to rise up her throat. She clamped her hand over her mouth and swallowed it back down. That guy still thought he could fuck her. She gulped a mouthful of cold coffee. She hadn't even taken the car. She wasn't going to let him touch her again. No way. She gripped the edge of her desk to stop her hands from shaking. There had to be a way to get him off her back. Nicole. She needed to call Nicole.

. . .

WHEN NICOLE LANDED at BWI Thurgood Marshall Airport, it was 4:30 p.m. local time. She'd slept three hours on the plane. Thank God for first class. The landing gate was standing room only with passengers heading back to San Francisco, and the concourse was busy, but she found a women's restroom with no line. While she was in the stall, she put her Nicole Carter wallet into her rolling carry-on bag and replaced it with her Caroline Webber wallet. She spotted a Caffeination coffee shop on her way toward the main terminal. As she stood in line for coffee, she checked her messages. There were two missed calls. She clicked on the first one.

"Yeah, hello?"

"I'm returning your call."

"You are. I've got your package."

"Call me tomorrow morning with a time and place."

"Will do."

She clicked on the second one.

"Travel Dreams."

"Lily?"

"Nicole. I tried to call you hours ago."

"Something came up. I'm out of town."

"Out of town?"

"Yeah. What do you need?"

Lily told her about her conversation with the guy from the parking lot. Nicole got her coffee and sat down at an empty gate. "We've got to be completely honest with each other if I'm going to help you."

"Okay."

"Would you have sex with this guy if you thought you could trust him to give you your bag?"

"No."

"And you don't think he'll just forget about you after a while?"

"I don't think so."

"So you can't just buy a new phone and get a new license?"

"He's got my address, and he says he knows where I work."

"Are you on friendly terms with a bartender at that bar?"

"Lucky Joe's?"

"Yeah."

"I know a few of the guys."

"Any women?"

"No."

"Makes it a little tougher, but it will work. Go to the bar. Tell the bartender that a guy tried to rape you in the parking lot. Tell him you were afraid to report it, but that some people helped you and you changed your mind, and you want to see the surveillance footage to see if it's good enough to press charges."

"How will that help me get my bag back?"

"If the footage is good, get a copy. Then you'll have something to trade. If not, see if you can get his car's license plate number, and we'll go forward from there."

"This is your plan?"

"You want your bag? You don't want to screw this guy, and you don't want to move? This is how you get it done. Of course, you could always just forget about it."

"I don't think I can do that."

"Then get the footage. And buy a cheap phone and text me your number so we can stay in touch." She glanced down the concourse. "Look, you can do this. Call me when you get the footage."

Nicole rolled her case out onto the sidewalk in front of the terminal. Passengers stood in clumps with their bags waiting for their rides while cars and minivans fought their way to the curb. The closest shuttle bus stop to the economy parking was off to the right. She put on her sunglasses. Lily and her easy, easy problems. She shook her head. She had to put Lily out of her mind. She needed to focus on Tony. How badly was he hurt? Were killers still after him? Every choice she made might be the one choice that made all the difference.

The shuttle bus jostled out of the terminal, down a one-way access road, and into a gated parking lot. The other passengers looked as if they were resigned to long lines and bad traffic. She got off at the last stop and pretended to adjust her bag while the last two passengers disappeared among the cars. Then she started down the nearest aisle, taking her time, looking for a car that was reasonably comfortable, handled well, and was as common as dirt. She stopped at a tan Toyota Camry with a standard license plate, glanced around, popped the door lock, and put her roller bag in the back. Then she hot-wired the ignition. Half a tank of gas. She made a left out of the airport and drove west toward Mitchellville. Forty minutes later, she pulled into a Target superstore parking lot, rode up and down the aisles until she found another Camry off in the far corner, and swapped out the license plates. An hour and a half later, she got off the interstate at the first Mitchellville exit.

She pulled into a strip mall, parked well away from the security cameras, and went into a Your Health Pharmacy. She bought a backpacker first aid kit, three bottles of Gatorade, a box of granola bars, six tubs of microwavable soup, a six-pack of water, a fifth of Jim Beam whiskey, and two cell phones. She used her Caroline Webber credit card. Then she got back on the interstate and got off on Sixty-third Street. It was just as Tony had described it. Seedy truck stop on one side of the divided highway and the motel, looking worse for wear, on the other side. She parked in front of his room and knocked on the door. The door cracked open, displaying the business end of a Glock.

"Love you, honey," she said.

The door swung open. Tony was standing in his boxer shorts, duct tape wrapped around his middle. He looked like a wino after a two-week bender.

She folded him into a hug. "You look like shit," she whispered.

He smiled. "You can't imagine how wonderful it is to see you."

"Get back in bed. I've got to unload the car."

She carried in the bags from the pharmacy and rolled in her carry-on bag. "How are you?"

"I'm okay, I think."

She got out the first aid kit and took his temperature. "Your temp's good. Do you want something to eat?"

"Fill me in first."

She handed him a Gatorade before she sat on the edge of the bed. "I got in touch with Billy before I left town."

"Not Zed?"

"Zed doesn't like women. Billy always takes care of me. I've heard from his guy. We'll have a couple of combat kits tomorrow. That's the good news."

"And the bad news?"

"You're going to the vet."

"Woof."

She activated her new phone and called the Happy Pets Clinic. The call rolled over to the automated message, which gave an emergency number. She called that.

"Danny Newberry."

"Billy told me to call you."

"I've been expecting your call."

"Can you come to us?"

"It would be better to meet at the clinic. Pull around the back. I'll let you in through the service door. You know the address?"

"We're on our way." She ended the call.

"So we're going to the vet's," Tony said.

"We need to get you dressed."

"I've got a change of clothes in my go bag."

She pulled a shirt and pants out of the go bag and helped him get dressed. "Can you walk to the car?"

"I made it this far. Grab my gun off the dresser."

She glanced out the motel room door. No one was in the parking lot. She walked Tony to the Camry and closed his door for him before she climbed into the driver's seat and input the address of Happy Pets Clinic into her smartphone. She took a right on Brockville Road, heading into town. A few more turns and they were on Washington Trail. Happy Pets was located in a strip of shops next to Painted Poodles Dog Groomers. Nicole drove through the empty parking lot to the service door at the back. As she helped Tony out of the car, the door opened. A tall black man stood in the threshold. "You the Missus?"

"Yes."

"And that's your man?"

"Yes. How do you know Billy?"

"He helped me sort out a problem. Come on."

Newberry led them down a hallway into what looked like a surgical suite. "The operating table is a little short—my largest patient is a Great Dane—but everything I need is in here." Newberry looked at him appraisingly. "Take your shirt and pants off."

Tony lay on the table in his boxer shorts. His ankles and feet hung off the end. Newberry slipped a surgical gown over his street clothes and put on throwaway gloves. "Let's have a look."

He cut away the duct tape to reveal a small hole seeping blood at the center of a large purple-and-yellow bruise. He swabbed the wound. "I've seen worse. I was a medic in the army."

"And now you're a vet," Tony said.

"I like animals. Can you roll up on your side?" Newberry looked at Tony's back. "Looks like it went through. Odd trajectory, like it was coming from below."

"Ricocheted up under my vest."

He pointed toward a doorway. "Better get an x-ray." He glanced at Nicole. "Help me navigate this table."

They rolled Tony into the x-ray room. Newberry took an x-ray of the wound area and pulled up the image on a computer. "No fragments. At least not close by. This looks good."

They rolled Tony back into the surgery. "You're a lucky guy. Two inches over, and I'd be sending you to the emergency room. I'm going to inject a local anesthetic, clean the wound, and stitch it up," Newberry said.

After he was finished, he taped a dressing on both sides of the wound. "Six weeks to full recovery. Stay out of the shower for four days. I'm going to give you some antibiotics. If you get any puss, give me a call. Stitches out in a week. No running or lifting for the next couple of weeks. It's probably going to hurt when the anesthetic wears off."

"Thanks, Doc." Tony pulled on his pants.

"What do we owe you?" Nicole asked.

Newberry shook his head. "This is between me and Billy." He walked them to the back door and switched on the outside light.

The wind had come up. Clouds were boiling in the night sky, and they could hear the traffic on the interstate in the distance. Nicole opened the passenger door for Tony. "I should have had Newberry put a GPS chip in you while I had you in there. Make you easier to find next time."

"You think there's going to be a next time?"

She got in the driver's seat and backed out from behind the clinic. "These jobs you've been picking have been nothing but trouble."

"I've been having a string of bad luck, no doubt about it."

"Bad luck?"

He grinned. "I thought with being shot and all, I'd get a few more days of peace before you reamed me a new one for being an idiot."

"Don't you think it's time to run?"

"I'm not running." He caught her up with what had happened.

"I told you not to trust Missy."

"I didn't trust her."

"She probably told them you were coming after them at the airport."

"All true."

"So why aren't we running?"

"Bastards killed Duke and Barker. Tried to kill me. Besides, that crooked Fed's reach is probably too long."

"Maybe they think you're dead."

"Maybe. Remember the El Paso job? Garcia—the good Fed— claims she can close that case if I bring her the blackmail info."

"It's not blackmail info."

"Yeah. It's probably stolen intel of some sort."

She took a right at the red light. "And she's not going to close that case. We'd need an FBI supervisor under our thumb to do that."

"Maybe. But I'm still not running. The crooked Fed, those other assholes, and let's not forget Missy."

"We could come back for Missy later."

"I'm not leaving."

"You've already got all the money."

He shook his head. "When I leave here, there's going to be less people looking for me than there are now and a lot more people dead who were trying to kill me."

"You're a stubborn bastard. If you hadn't been in such a hurry to get even, you wouldn't have gotten ambushed. You know that, don't you?"

"Rub it in."

"You're right. I'm rubbing it in. You're not going to get me killed."

He smiled. "So you're going to help me?"

"Of course I'm going to help you. It's always us. Period."

"I love to hear you say that." He leaned back in his seat, watching her drive, a satisfied look on his face.

After a few minutes, she said, "What are you thinking about?"

"Nobody knows you're here. We're going to keep it that way. Tomorrow, if I'm doing okay, we're going to start shaking the trees. And you're going to see what falls out."

BACK AT THE MOTEL, after Tony went to sleep, Nicole watched him in the light that slanted into the room from the half-open bathroom door. Some food, some medical attention, some TLC, and he already looked much better. The only other time he'd been shot was when she'd shot him to keep Buddy from killing him, and that had been a similar situation. He'd gotten in too big a hurry to read the tells properly. She brushed his hair back off his forehead. Her pretty boy. She sipped her whiskey. But when he got on a roll, he was unstoppable. He could tell any lie and steal anything from anybody. They had so much fun together. But what about her other boy?

She set down her drink and picked up her phone. It was still early on the West Coast. She couldn't put it off any longer. She speed-dialed Denison. The phone rang four times before he picked up.

"Hey, sweetie," she said.

"How are you?"

"I'm fine. Everything is fine. I got Tony all fixed up."

"When are you coming home?"

"A couple of days of nursing should get the job done."

"You aren't doing anything crazy?"

"No, I'm just looking after Tony."

"Good."

"How's Lily?"

"I haven't heard from her," he said.

"That's probably a good sign."

"Or a very bad one."

"She's not your problem."

He sighed. "I miss you already. This is the first night you've been away since you came here."

"Don't worry, Jimmy. In a few days I'll be back."

"We'll find something for you to do—something you like. I know a career counselor."

She laughed. "Now you're teasing me."

"No, really, you've got amazing people skills. We'll find something where you can be anonymous, use your skills, enjoy some excitement."

"You don't have to worry, sweetie. I'm coming back to you. We'll figure things out."

"Okay, then."

"I love you."

"I love you too."

FRIDAY MORNING, Tony and Nicole sat in a cracked vinyl booth in the window of the Trucker's Delight diner. The air smelled of old cooking grease and burned bacon. The morning rush was made up of four truckers and a mom and dad with two young kids who were pondering their location on an iPad. Tony and Nicole were eating pancakes and eggs and keeping an eye on the front of their motel across the divided highway. Nicole had already packed up the motel room and wiped it down. She had found them another motel, a

Quality Inn, using her Caroline Webber credit card. Their plan was breakfast, clothes shopping for Tony, and picking up the heavy gear from Billy's guy. Then off to the new motel. Tony would rest up while Nicole scouted out Missy. If she wasn't dead, she was their best hope of gaining information on the bad guys.

Tony set his cutlery on his plate and pushed the plate away. "I am so full I could fall asleep right here."

Nicole dipped the corner of her toast in her egg yolk. "I've eaten better."

"Don't start. You've been in San Francisco too long. This breakfast is reasonably decent for most of the US."

She rolled her eyes.

Tony took a sip of coffee. "Time to start making it rain." He called Missy. The phone rang, but no one answered and the voice mailbox was full. "So much for Missy."

"You didn't think she'd pick up, did you?"

He took out the phone Garcia had given him and clicked on the only phone number.

Garcia picked up on the second ring. "I thought you were dead."

"A common misperception."

"You got anything for me?"

"Hang on. I'm texting you a pic of the guys from the airport who picked up Clemens." He looked at the face of the phone, found the picture in his cloud storage, then sent it to her phone number. He put the phone back to his ear. "Your guy—the one who has the envelope —is in the middle."

"Yeah, I know him. The other two guys I don't. And Clemens was found in a dumpster in an alley. Bad break. He was working for us."

"So these fellas have been taking out the trash from the very beginning?"

"You've got a funny way of talking about the good guys."

"Your case going up in smoke? Who do you have left to testify?"

"Let me worry about that."

"You remember that woman who was with me?"

"Yeah?"

"She turn up dead?"

"Haven't seen her. Why? You looking for her? What do you want her for?"

"We going to start being honest with each other?"

"I'm still waiting on that envelope."

"If you want that envelope, all you have to do is talk with your colleague."

"You're very funny. Get me that envelope, and you'll get your get-out-of-jail-free card."

"Now who's funny?"

"I'll be in touch."

Tony put the phone away. "Clemens is dead, and Missy is probably still on the loose."

"So we stick with our plan?"

"Yeah."

Nicole glanced at the check and put some money on the table.

DURING LUNCH, Lily went back to Lucky Joe's. In the daylight, without music, it was just another dimly lit, rundown neighborhood bar that smelled of sour beer, dirty clothes, and wasted dreams. Four retired guys were gathered in the back corner. Big Eddie was sitting on a stool behind the bar, wheezing with every breath. He smiled when he saw her and slid onto his feet. "Hey, girl. Look at you." He gestured toward her clothes. "Didn't make you for the office type. What you drinking?"

"Hey, Eddie. Nothing for me. The reason I'm here—could you do me a favor?"

He wiped the bar with a rag. "Favor, huh? Depends on what it is."

She stood up on her toes to lean over the bar toward him. He bent down. "I was here on Tuesday."

"Cowboy band."

"Two guys jumped me in the parking lot."

The look in his eye said that he thought she might be trying to shake him down. "No shit."

"A couple came out. Scared them off. They drove me home. I was so flustered I didn't call the police. I mean, it was crazy."

He nodded.

"But now, I think maybe I should. I just don't know if it would do any good."

"You point those guys out next time they're here, they won't bother anybody else."

"I appreciate that."

"No problem."

"It's just that I was wondering if I could see the parking lot video. If it's clear what's happening, then I'd have evidence for the cops."

"That video is private property."

"I know."

"And this neighborhood has been going downhill. Could give this place a black eye."

"But if girls knew you were going to protect them, that you were going to have a no-tolerance policy for jerks, that could be good for business."

"Maybe." He patted the back of her hand. "I like you, Lily. I'd like to think we were friends. So let's take a look at the video. I'm not promising anything, but let's just take a look."

He turned toward the back corner. "Mikey." One of the retired guys looked up. "Watch the bar for a few minutes."

Big Eddie led the way into the back room. A Kmart desk with a computer on it was crammed into a corner next to a stack of liquor boxes. He sat down in the chair and opened the video recording program. "Last Tuesday." He pulled up the day. "About what time?"

"It was early. Ten, ten thirty."

She moved up to stand behind him. He clicked on the 10:00 p.m. marker. "Okay. Here we go." The video shot forward at triple speed. When Lily came out into the parking lot, Big Eddie slowed the video to normal. The video was black and white, and the lighting wasn't very good. "That's you, isn't it?"

"Yeah."

She was walking up the parking lot. When she stopped by the

BMW, Shaved Head and Comb-over moved into the picture. She knew it was them, remembered her fear, but the video was too poor to identify them. "Can you sharpen the image?"

He shook his head. "If I zoom in, it just gets blurrier. This is just to scare off burglars and car thieves."

"Stop there."

He stopped the video. Shaved Head had her pinned against the car. She could feel his hands on her. Her stomach rolled.

Big Eddie muttered, "Sorry bastard."

But in the video, Shaved Head was impossible to identify. He could have been anybody. She looked down at the trunk of the car. The surface of the license plate was bright. The numbers were dark. She thought she could make out most of them. She pulled a scrap of paper from her pocket and wrote down what she saw without Big Eddie noticing.

"There's nothing here," she said.

Big Eddie swiveled his chair. "Tough break, kid. I wish the video could have helped. Those assholes got a beating coming. You point them out, I'll put some guys on them."

"Thanks for taking the time."

Lily squinted in the bright light as she stepped out onto the street in front of the bar. She found Nicole's number in the address book on her phone. "Hey, it's me. Is this a bad time?"

"No. I've got a few minutes. What's up?"

Lily told her what had happened. "Tough break," Nicole said. "But maybe we can work with the license plate number. There's two numbers you're not sure of. But one of them is either a five or an S. That's not really that many options. I know a guy who can track these numbers, provide info on all the possible license plates so we can figure out which one is your guy. Then we'll know who he is, where he lives, everything about him. If that's what you want."

"Can't we do something simpler?"

"You could set up a meeting with him like you're going to screw him and then send some guys to beat on him."

"I can't do that."

"Then you need some leverage. You can't get it if you don't know who he is."

"Okay. Call your friend."

"It'll cost a few bucks."

"How much?"

"Depends on how hard it is to track the numbers. Maybe a couple hundred. Maybe more. You got yourself in a jam. If you want peace of mind, it's going to take some money to straighten things out."

Lily held her phone against her chest. She could hear Shaved Head's voice in her mind. Even if she moved, changed jobs, she'd never know when he might turn up, catch her somewhere in the dark, knowing she wouldn't call the police. She couldn't live like this. Always afraid. But would Nicole's plan work? "I hear what you're saying. It makes sense. But how do you know hackers? How do you know who to call and what to plan? I mean, going for that joyride is the most illegal thing I've ever done."

"Lily, I don't have time to share my life story or convince you of anything. Either you trust me or you don't. What do you want to do?"

"Okay. Call your guy."

"Give me the license plate number. I'll be back in touch when I have the info."

"WHO WAS THAT?" Tony asked.

They were sitting in the Camry facing out of a picnic spot in the back end of Memorial Park, the largest park in Mitchellville. Tall evergreen bushes shielded their right side, and a thick grove of pine provided cover from the right. Tony's Glock lay in his lap.

"Lily." Nicole explained what had happened.

"I told you. Picking up strays. It'll be the death of you. You should have turned her away at the door."

"Even if I had wanted to, I couldn't have explained it to James."

"You've got him wrapped around your finger. He would have believed anything you said."

"Tony, this is a big problem for Lily, even if it's nothing to us. She got into this problem doing what I showed her. I'm just going to guide her through it."

"And how much will she end up knowing about you?"

"That's not a problem."

"It's always a problem. If she's not with us, it's a problem."

A rusty red-and-white Bronco came down the road toward them and flashed its lights. "Here he comes." Nicole flashed back.

"We're not done talking about this," Tony said.

The Bronco backed in next to them. A middle-aged woman wearing a sleeveless button-up shirt and a cowboy hat lowered her window. Tony lowered his window with his left hand and held his pistol in his right.

"Howdy," the woman said. "Pretty day, ain't it? Who are you folks?"

"I'm the Traveling Man."

"And I'm the Missus. Who are you?"

She smiled. "Billy sends his regards. Your gear is in the back."

Nicole popped the trunk on the Camry, and the woman lifted the back on the Bronco. Two short cases, a long case, and a bag sat in the cargo space. She opened one of the short cases. It contained an AR-15 rifle, a Glock 17, and a Kevlar vest. "Other one's the same." She opened the long case. A sniper rifle sat in the foam.

"Quality gear," Tony said.

"And here's the tech." Inside the bag were communications head-sets and tracking devices.

"Great," Nicole said.

They moved the gear into the Camry.

"Thanks for the business," the woman said.

"Tell Billy we appreciate the help," Tony said. "You go first."

They watched the Bronco leave the picnic spot and disappear down the road into the woods. Then Nicole drove off the road and into the park, bouncing over the terrain and meandering through the trees until she came to another road. A kid's birthday party was being set up under a shelter near the park entrance—bright banner and balloons tied to the posts—when they turned out of the park. No one was following them.

"That's the amount of care you should always take," Tony said. "Not trusting some stranger, no matter who sent them."

"Yeah. Or maybe you shouldn't go off half-cocked just because you think you know what you're doing."

"I'm just saying that doing some dirt with someone is not the same as knowing them."

"And who had to come out here to save who?" Nicole replied.

"This time."

"I think maybe it's time for your nap."

MIDAFTERNOON, Nicole sat in the Camry across the street and down the block from Missy's condo. Most of the on-street parking was full. The row houses were all newly renovated and tastefully landscaped with small trees and bright-green shrubs. No one had been in or out of the condo in over an hour, and no one appeared to be watching it. Nicole was wearing a black pantsuit with an open-collar pink shirt. If anyone asked, she was a real estate agent. She got out of the car with a small bag over her shoulder and a clipboard in her hand. She walked purposefully down the sidewalk, crossed the street at an angle, and strode up the steps to Missy's row house. She reached in her bag as if she were grabbing her keys, brought out her lock picks, and was inside in a matter of seconds.

The row house was decorated in an arty, contemporary style. Not Missy at all. Nicole moved quickly through the rooms, glancing in the closets as she went. There was no landline phone with a voice mail to listen to, no desk piled with papers to sort through, no mess to indicate that somebody else had searched the house. She called Tony. "Nothing here. The girlfriend must be a good three inches taller than Missy."

"Have you gone by her gallery?"

"That's my next stop. I came here first."

"I reached out to Kevin with that license plate number."

"Why not just use Billy?"

"Don't want anyone knowing too much about our business. Besides, Kevin owes us a favor. It'll be cheaper for your girl."

"Thanks."

Nicole drove downtown into the shopping district. The gallery—American Moderns—was located midblock between an antique furniture shop and Zelda Jane's Interior Design Studio. Two women's torsos, sculpted in white clay, were on display in the window. Nicole pushed through the glass door. Large abstract paintings hung on the side and back walls. The interior was filled with sculptures, while jewelry was in a case at the back.

"Good afternoon." A young woman in a black dress, her right arm tattooed from the back of her hand all the way up to her shoulder, smiled as she walked toward her.

"Is Betty here?"

"She's on a buying trip. Is there anything I can help you with?"

"Do you know when she'll be back?"

She shook her head.

"I'll try back another time. Tell her Carrie Traveler stopped by to see her girlfriend."

When she came back out onto the street, she noticed a guy sitting in a pickup truck where he could keep an eye on the gallery. Military haircut, sunglasses, cigarette in one hand—the kind of guy who would be completely at home in a third-world hot spot. Nicole sauntered along, playing the window-shopping game. As she walked, she got out her phone and took a picture of the window display in a dress shop. Then, as she moved to put the phone away, she took pictures of the guy and the license plate of his truck. She walked around the block to get back to her car so that she wouldn't have to walk past him and risk drawing attention to herself.

She called Tony. "The girlfriend is in hiding. A probable merc is watching the gallery."

"So Missy doesn't trust her playmates. You leave a message?"

"Uh-huh. Should I start tailing the merc?"

"No. We don't want the bad guys to catch sight of you. They don't get to see you until it's too late."

"I'm headed back to you. What kind of takeout do you want?"

"Chinese would be good." There was a pause. "And pick up some beer."

Nicole pulled into an alley to turn around. She took a left at the stop light. The traffic was stop and go. It seemed like everyone was trying to get out of the downtown business district at the same time. She took a right and found herself stuck in bumper-to-bumper traffic on a one-way street. Her Nicole phone rang. It was Denison.

"Hey, honey." She tried to sound nonchalant.

"Is this a good time?" Denison asked.

"Absolutely. I'm stuck in traffic."

"What are you doing?"

"Getting some takeout."

"Really? You're not just saying that?"

"Relax, Jimmy. I'm not interacting with any of the players. I'm just taking care of Tony."

"How is he?"

"He's doing great. Getting his strength back. It's only going to be a few more days, then I'll be back home."

"Good."

"How are you?"

"Okay. Running into some NIMBY issues with the new facility, but nothing we can't handle. Bell sent some pictures of the wedding venue last night."

"What did she end up choosing?"

"The university's convention center. They had a cancellation. It's next to the arboretum, so there'll be lots of great outdoor pictures. It's a turnkey deal—everything's included. She says that the food's not great, but it's as good as you can get for a hundred people out there."

"No one will remember the food."

"That's for sure. Did you see her dress?"

"Yeah. She sent me a pic. A little retro for me, but it looks great on her."

"It's sort of modeled on her mom's," Denison replied.

Nicole pulled into the parking at the Szechwan House. "What's the rest of your day look like?"

"Nothing special. What about you?"

"I'm going to eat some Chinese and watch TV."

"I miss you."

"I miss you too. See you in a few days."

She got out of the car and started across the parking lot to the restaurant. He could play a good game, but she could hear the worry in his voice. He couldn't quite believe that she was doing nothing dangerous, and he was right. But there was no way she was going to tell him what she was really up to. This wasn't his world. He wouldn't understand.

LATER THAT EVENING, at the Quality Inn, after they'd checked over their new gear, loaded the guns, and tested the tech, Nicole inspected Tony's wounds while he sat in his boxer shorts on the edge of the bed. "These look good. Only the edges of the stitches are red."

"Feels a lot better."

"Antibiotics probably help."

She put a large Band-Aid over each side of the wound. "There you go."

He leaned forward to kiss her.

"None of that. We're not going to start anything that could tear your stitches."

"Fucking Missy Grey." He scooted back against the headboard.

Nicole came around the bed and scooted up beside him.

"You talking to Denison?" he asked.

"Yes."

"How's he taking it?"

"For starters, in his mind, every job is like Nohamay City or Cricket Bay."

"So he's churning."

"Mentally, he knew you might call, but emotionally, he was convinced it would never happen."

"Bouncing off the walls."

"On top of that, he knows I'm having adjustment problems, so he's afraid I won't come back. Offered to set me up with a career counselor."

Tony chuckled. "That guy is a problem solver. That's his default mode."

"Yeah, he's so sweet. That's the one way he's just like you."

Tony ignored her last statement. "But he's right. You've got to get integrated into that life if it's going to stick."

"I'll probably take him up on his offer just to calm him down. But the real problem is that pretending to do a thing so you can steal from someone is a lot more fun than actually doing a thing."

"Especially when you're pretending to do a thing so you can steal from a crook."

She nodded. "Change of subject. Are you finally ready to give up on this BS? Missy's a dead end."

"I don't think so. I think she's still on the move."

"Doesn't mean we can find her."

"You left a message for the girlfriend, didn't you?"

"Yeah."

"Not giving up yet. I'm Missy's best bet to stay alive, and she knows it. She'll be in touch."

7

TIGHTROPE

Midmorning, Nicole and Tony were sitting at the table by the window in their motel room, playing cards and keeping an eye on the parking lot. They could hear a cleaner vacuuming the room next door. Their car was packed to leave. They'd been to breakfast at a crowded McDonald's two exits south. Now they were waiting, hoping Missy's girlfriend had relayed the message. Tony's phone rang. He glanced at the number and smiled.

"How you doing, sugar?"

"I want to talk," Missy said.

"I bet."

"You okay?"

"Still breathing. I've had plenty of time to make my to-do list."

"Hey, no one was supposed to get hurt. You guys were supposed to get the envelope and give it to Chen. That's all."

"But that's not what happened."

"I know."

"So why are you calling me? I appreciate your apology—if that's what it is. But it doesn't let you off the hook, not by a long shot. There's you, and there's your girl."

"Slow down now. There's no reason to make threats. I called you, okay? I can't trust those guys, and it looks like my guy doesn't have the juice to keep them off me."

"And you're hoping I can help."

"Who did you send to the gallery?"

"That was a cute little trick, wasn't it?"

"Look, we've got the same problem. We could be on the same side."

"So we meet, and you tell me everything you know about these assholes, including your boy."

"You promise not to kill me?"

"You stupid enough to take my word?"

"Hightower Park, benches next to the playground, tomorrow at one o'clock."

"See you there." He set down his phone.

"So what's the deal?" Nicole asked.

"We're in business. I'm meeting Missy tomorrow."

"By yourself?"

"She sounded like she was really afraid. She's going to give up that crew in hopes I won't kill her."

"That doesn't mean it's not a setup."

"But if it's not, I'm well on my way to killing all of those bastards. Let's think this through." He was quiet for a moment. "We're meeting in Hightower Park. You're going to be set up with the sniper rifle. If you see any of those guys, you start shooting. That's my insurance policy. But if she's ready to deal, we'll find out everything she knows about that crew. And then when she leaves, you tail her."

"You're going to be wearing a vest."

"Only an idiot would go to this meeting without Kevlar and a gun."

BACK IN SAN FRANCISCO BAY, Sanders sat in his BMW in the parking lot of All Stars dance studio, playing solitaire on his smartphone. The parking lot was full. The sun was hot. Two moms and a dad were sitting on benches by the entrance chatting, but Sanders didn't mix with the other dance parents. That was his wife's job. He won his game and glanced at the time. Twenty more minutes. Next year, when his daughter could drive, he'd never have to come here again. It couldn't happen soon enough. One of the moms got up and stretched her arms over her head. She was a fine-looking specimen—thin, athletic, no cellulite yet. Her daughter must be one of the grade-schoolers, or she was nineteen when she pushed out her first.

His mind wandered to the car thief. She was a tasty tidbit. He hadn't heard back from her. Was she ignoring him, thinking that he'd just forget about her debt? He was going to make sure she was so intimidated that she would never tell anyone what had happened. And if she'd sleep with him in the meantime, so much the better. He took her phone out of his glove box. Password-protected. She could call him, but he couldn't call her. He knew where she lived, but there was no landline associated with that address. And he knew where she worked. There was a business card in her bag. Did she work on Saturdays? He took out his own phone and called the number.

"Travel Dreams."

"Hello, Lily. You haven't called me back yet. Your friends are beginning to wonder why a man is answering your phone. Maybe they think we're dating."

"You better leave me alone."

"Or what? You going to call the police? You going to tell them how I ended up with your handbag?"

"It was a mistake, okay?"

"It certainly turned into one. We're going to get together. You're going to give me what I want, and maybe I'll give you your bag back. Or I could turn it in to the police."

"It's too late for that."

"I'm the one with the authority. And the witness. Who are you?"

"Leave me alone."

"You know what you need to do."

He ended the call. Getting into her head was so easy. How many times would he get to fuck her before he was finally tired of her?

. . .

LILY SET HER PHONE DOWN. Why had she done it? It seemed crazy just thinking about it now. She looked at her computer screen. She had two sets of itineraries to finish before noon, but she couldn't focus. She needed coffee. She pushed away from her desk. Why had she thought that stealing the car keys was a good idea? She went down the hall into the break room. The coffee pot was half-empty. She poured a cup and added two sugars. That guy was the worst sort of creep. There was no way she was going to sleep with him.

Her officemate Chrissie came into the break room, a bottle of ibuprofen in her hand. "Hey, Lily," she said. She got a cup of water from the watercooler and downed two ibuprofen. "I've got that sharp pain behind my left eye. No more rosé wine." She pushed her messy blonde curls out of her face. "What's up with you? You okay? You need an ibuprofen?"

Lily shook her head. "I'm fine."

"Late night?"

"Yeah."

"Me too. We were all at Trixie's for women's night. Where were you?"

"Long story. Tell you about it later. I've got to get back to my desk."

She went back into the front office. Had Nicole found out anything? Anything that could help? She got out the Walmart phone Nicole had told her to buy.

"Hey," Nicole said. "How are you?"

"Not good. He called me at work. He threatened to call the cops. He—"

"Slow down. My friend came back with a pile of info. We're going to figure out who he is, and we're going to shut him down."

"Really?"

"Yeah. I'm in the middle of something. It's going to take a couple more days. So just stall him and stay out of his way. As soon as I get back, we'll put together a plan to deal with him."

"How can you be so confident?"

"Just do what I say."

"I don't see how—"

"Just stall him. I'll see you in a few days."

She sat down at her desk. How could Nicole be so sure? What did she really know about her? What kind of person was she? Chitchatting. Hustling drinks. Going for a joyride. The wedding reception flashed through her mind. The car key game had been a step too far, but at the time it had just seemed like a harmless dare. Something with no downside at all. But hiring a hacker? That was completely illegal, and she'd agreed to it because it seemed like the only way to get leverage on this guy. What would Nicole propose next? What would happen if the police caught them doing whatever Nicole had in mind?

ON SUNDAY at 1:00 p.m., Tony stood on a corner across the street from Hightower Park. The sun was warm. Joggers, dog walkers, and couples moved along the park paths. Families were sprawled on blankets with their picnics. An elderly woman was throwing bits of bread to the ducks at the pond. The playground was full of squealing children, the parents standing at the edges watching the fun. Missy was sitting on a bench. Tony took another look around. He couldn't see anyone who was as dangerous as he was. He glanced up to the roof of a ten-story apartment building catty-corner to his position and saw the glint of Nicole's rifle scope. He breathed in and out slowly. It was time to move. He crossed at the crosswalk and strolled across the grass to the playground.

"Missy." He smiled and sat down beside her.

"Kevlar's a bit much, don't you think?"

"I've got trust issues. Let's start with this picture." He took out his phone and showed her the picture he took at the airport.

"Clemens you know."

"He's dead," Tony replied.

"I'm not surprised. Robertson I've known for years. He's been a steady client. The older guy is named French; he's a military contractor, I think. The other guy is one of his. I don't know what their game is other than what you already know."

"But you were working me."

"Robertson promised me it was just to keep you out of the mix, that nothing would happen to you."

"And you believed him?"

"He's always been straight with me."

A kickball rolled over to the bench. Tony stopped it with his foot, then scooped it up and tossed it back toward a group of kids who were close by.

"This can go two ways. I can assume you're still trying to play me, and I can deal with you and your girlfriend—"

"Betty's got nothing to do with this."

"Or I can believe you're being straight with me, in which case you're willing to do your part to make this right."

"What do I have to do?"

Tony raised up his arms as if he were stretching, Nicole's signal to come down off the roof. "You're going to set up a face-to-face with Robertson."

"Do I look that stupid?"

"I'll have your back. We need Robertson if we're going to find French and his crew. You're going to put a transmitter on him."

"How will I do that?"

"You're a big girl. Find a way to get it done."

"And then I'm out?"

"So far as the heavy lifting."

"Meaning?"

"I know you're not a killer."

"I could drive you when you go for them."

"We'll see where our trust level is when the time comes. You get in touch with Robertson. I'll get the transmitter. We'll meet at seven at the Gravy Boat Diner."

"That place over on Glendale?"

"Yeah."

"See you then."

Missy took the path around the playground and cut across the park, skirting the pond. Tony got out his phone and speed-dialed Nicole. "You got her?"

"She's getting in a blue Audi. Got to go."

NICOLE SLIPPED into an on-street handicap parking space in her Camry and watched Missy get into her Audi about four cars ahead of her. What she pulled out, Nicole followed. Away from Hightower Park and the nearby restaurants, the downtown was Sunday afternoon deserted and the traffic was sparse, so Nicole had to stay well back, driving like a tourist who wasn't sure of her destination. After Missy took a right turn, Nicole hid behind a city bus for three blocks. When the bus stopped, Nicole pulled right up behind Missy at the red light and looked down as if she were checking her smartphone. Missy took a left toward the freeway. The traffic picked up. Nicole stayed three cars back. Missy barreled up the entrance ramp, sped down the beltway to the next exit ramp, dropped her speed as if she were getting off, and then hit the gas and blew past that exit.

At the following exit, she got off on Kennedy Boulevard and drove back into town, staying just under the speed limit. Nicole was still behind her. Missy drove into a neighborhood of newly built condos and parked on the street. Then she walked two blocks and crossed the street into a neighborhood of three-story walk-up apartments near Mitchellville College. A bearded guy dressed in a lumberjack shirt and jeans was sitting on the steps in front of one building. When he saw her, he pushed himself up off the steps. They shook hands, and he ushered her into the building.

Nicole wrote down the building address and drove back to the motel. Tony was sitting up on the bed when she came through the door.

"What's up with Missy?"

"Looks like she's staying with some hipsters."

"Everybody owes her favors. As long as she thinks she's safe, we know where to find her."

Nicole kicked off her shoes and padded over to the minifridge for a bottle of water. "Are you really going to let her off the hook?"

"She does her part, I won't kill her girlfriend, but I still haven't made up my mind about her."

MISSY STOOD in the living room of Barry's apartment. Old wood floors, sagging sofa, a poster advertising a street party last year, dirty windows looking out onto the street. He came back in from the kitchen and handed her a bottle of beer.

"When does everyone get back?" she asked.

"Jackie gets off work at five. Miguel and Sophie? I haven't seen them all weekend. Doesn't matter. Nobody will care if you crash on the couch for a few days."

"Great."

"We are only talking about a few days?"

"Maybe not even that long." She took a pull off the bottle. "Don't worry. I know how to take care of a friend. I'll make sure you meet that guy."

"Thanks, Missy."

"I've got to make a private phone call, so I'm going into the bathroom."

"*Mi casa, su casa.*"

She went down the narrow hallway to the tiny bathroom. There was a small window over the tub and peeling paint on the ceiling. It was as depressing as a prison cell. She put the lid down on the toilet and sat. It was time to pick a side. She got out her phone.

"Robertson?"

"Damn it, Missy, where have you been? Why did you run? I had you covered."

"I don't trust those bastards you're running with. They could have accidently killed me on purpose."

"I can protect you."

"I think we've had this conversation before. By the way, my guy is still alive."

"Are you sure?"

"Breathing and talking."

"Do you know where he is?"

"Meet me at Lysistrata at nine."

"The lesbian bar downtown?"

"The very one. By yourself. And Robertson? No guns."

She put her phone away and went back out to the living room. Barry was looking out the window with his beer in his hand. "Woman across the way does yoga in her underwear."

"She know you're looking?"

"She must. Jackie noticed her first."

Through the window across the street, they watched a slim dark-haired woman dressed only in a bra and panties working her way through a sun salutation.

"Jackie's got a great eye for a straight girl," Missy said. An image of Betty, naked, her robe hanging loose from her shoulders, flashed through her mind.

"You're not kidding."

"You haven't told anyone I'm staying here?"

"No one. Jackie won't even find out until she gets here."

"I really appreciate your help, Barry."

ROBERTSON and French stood in the living room of a little farmhouse just outside the city limits. A For Sale sign stood in the front yard by the gravel driveway. Their trucks were parked in the backyard, and French's men, three burly mercenaries, were unloading cots and equipment into the empty bedrooms. Robertson put away his phone.

"Who was that?" French asked.

"Missy."

He chuckled. "She decide to quit being afraid?"

"The safecracker is still alive."

"That's not possible. He was gut shot."

"Yeah, well, once you decided to kill him you should have made sure."

"You know we couldn't risk staying there any longer than we did. She know where he is?"

"She's spooked. I'm meeting her tonight."

"I'll put a couple of my guys on her."

"There's no need to do that. She's my CI."

"Paul, we're not going to hurt her. You have my word. But we have to find this guy. If she's too afraid to tell us, then we need to follow her to him. It's the quickest way. Once that troublemaker is dealt with, we're in the clear. It's that simple."

AT 7:00 P.M., Tony and Missy sat drinking coffee in a booth in the back corner of the Gravy Boat Diner. The restaurant was almost empty. An elderly couple were picking over the meatloaf and mashed potatoes they were sharing, and two teenage girls were drinking milkshakes and giggling over something they were looking at on a smartphone. Tony had a clear sight line out into the parking lot, and the door to the kitchen was only a few steps to his right. The back door was alarmed. Nicole was in her car across the street at the closed mechanic's shop. If Missy had set him up, she'd be dead before she got to the street corner.

He sipped his coffee. "You're still alive. You must have a great safe house."

"I'm on the move."

"We think alike." He passed her a small box containing the transmitter.

She peeked inside. "It's tiny."

"Welcome to the twenty-first century. GPS tracking. See the switch?"

"Yeah."

"Turn it on ahead of time. He's a suit guy, isn't he?"

She nodded.

"Put it in the inside pocket of his suit jacket."

"How am I supposed to do that?"

"Think about how free you're going to feel when all these assholes are dead. You'll find a way."

She slipped the box into her jacket pocket. "You know Lysistrata?"

"Yeah."

"We're meeting at nine."

"Smart. French's guys will have a hard time blending in."

"I'm going to get there at eight."

"We'll be ready. Just make sure he's wearing the transmitter when he leaves."

She slid out of the booth and walked away. Tony sat there sipping his coffee as he watched her cross the parking lot to a Toyota Yaris. He bet it was newly stolen. No flies on her. Which was why she couldn't be trusted. She'd say anything or do anything to get out from under. One step at a time. Either she was going to put the transmitter on Robertson or she was going to make an excuse. And that would tell him everything he needed to know.

MISSY SAT on a stool at the bar in Lysistrata. Even though it was Sunday, most of the tables and the seats at the bar were occupied. A folk duo played from a raised area in the back corner. The lights were dim, and the customers, women with a smattering of men, whispered to one another as they sipped their drinks. Missy didn't like being here on business—the place wasn't loud enough or dark enough, and the bartender was certainly going to remember a middle-aged man in a dark suit—but safety was her most important concern. No one was going to pull a woman out of this bar. And she'd easily escape out the back if someone were watching the front.

Robertson came through the door. She waved. He looked as out of place as humanly possible. She turned to the bartender, a tattooed woman in a sleeveless top. "Give me another Chardonnay. My dad will have a whiskey on the rocks."

As he approached, she stood, took the transmitter from her pocket, hugged him as if she were frisking him, and slipped the device into his inside suit coat pocket.

"Was that really necessary?" he asked.

She shrugged. "I ordered you a whiskey."

"Thanks."

She got back up on her stool.

He leaned in close. "So tell me about the safecracker."

"Your guys tagged him."

"How bad?"

"He's not moving too fast."

"So where is he?"

"I don't know, but he's willing to walk away if you are."

"Must be shot pretty bad. Find out where he's staying."

"Why? Why should I do that? You told me nobody else was going to get hurt."

"That boat sailed when you couldn't keep him from following us from the airport."

"Paul, really? You're going to try to put this on me?"

"Missy, take a breath. You're not some stranger who knows too much. You're with me. We have history. I'm not going to let anything happen to you."

"What about French?"

"He has a tendency to overreact. I admit it. But once the safecracker is dealt with, there's no more loose ends."

"You're not inspiring confidence."

"Just find out where he's staying. He can't come after you if he's dead, and I'll kick in an extra two thousand."

"Okay, I'll see what I can do."

"You do that."

Robertson drained his glass and left the bar. Missy sat nursing her wine. The folk duo took a break. She wondered what Betty was doing. She should call her. She couldn't have her start thinking that she didn't really love her and was just living off her, but first she needed to deal with Tony. She got out her phone. "Hey, Tony."

"Yeah?"

"It's done."

"Great. If I need you, I'll let you know."

He ended the call. She sipped her wine. Was it really done? Could he really deal with the mercs? He couldn't possibly be planning to kill Robertson. Kill a Fed and you wind up dead. No, he was out of his depth, overmatched. He should have run. She wouldn't be hearing from him again. She called Betty.

"Hey, beautiful."

"I am so glad to hear your voice. What's that noise in the background? Where are you?"

"Lysistrata."

"Without me?"

"It's strictly business. What are you doing?"

"Hiding in the guest bedroom. C.J. has been driving me insane. She makes my OC seem completely normal. I don't even think my brother is listening to her half the time."

"What about the kids?"

"They're monsters."

She laughed.

"I'm not kidding. They're sugar-fueled advertisements for sterilization."

"I miss you."

"When are we going home?"

"Soon."

"That's too long."

"We could meet somewhere."

"Where?"

"What's the name of that hotel on Beech Street?"

"That dump?"

"This is what I'm reduced to. The bed can't be that bad."

Betty signed. "I'll text you with a room number."

ROBERTSON LEFT the Lysistrata parking lot in a Ford Explorer with Nicole and Tony, dressed in dark clothes, trailing after him in the Camry. It was a clear night. The traffic thinned out as they left the commercial district. Tony was following the transmitter on a GPS map on his phone. After Robertson took a right turn, Nicole dropped back a block. Robertson drove west, keeping just above the speed limit, driving as if he didn't have a care in the world. As they reached the edge of town, the houses were farther and farther apart. Finally, Robertson turned down a gravel road. Nicole and Tony pulled off on the shoulder, turned off their headlights, and waited, keeping track of Robertson's progress on the map. He came to a stop.

They lowered the car windows and drove slowly down the gravel road by the light of the stars, listening for any noises that might mean trouble. Up ahead to the right, they saw light shining out of the front windows of a little house, illuminating the Explorer parked in the front drive. Nicole turned left into the weeds, rolled over a shallow ditch, and parked up against a farm field fence. They opened the trunk, got out the AR-15 rifles, checked the magazines, and then started across the road, rifles at the ready. Tony felt relaxed, at peace with himself and the world. He took Nicole's hand and whispered in her ear, "I always get that good feeling when I'm on a job with you."

She kissed his cheek.

They crept up to the house, staying out of the light. Tony peeked through the front window into the living room. No one. They slipped around the left side, staying low to the ground. At the next window, Tony saw Robertson, French, and the thick-necked guy from the airport standing in the kitchen. Tony and Nicole squatted under the window to listen.

"She's onboard," Robertson said. "You've got no reason to tail her. She's going to come through."

"If that's the case, Rick and Gary are just there to protect her," French said.

"She's going to call as soon as she knows where he is."

"Then you've got nothing to worry about."

"Keep me in the loop."

The front door slammed. Nicole crawled back to the corner and saw the Explorer drive away. In the meantime, Tony peeked into the backyard. There were two trucks parked on the grass. Tony and Nicole met back at the kitchen window. They could hear French speaking. "Robertson's tougher than he looks. But if he can't let that lesbian go, he's not going to make it."

"Yes, sir," Thick Neck replied.

"I'm going to pick up the passports. You stay here."

French went out the back door and drove away in one of the trucks. Tony looked at Thick Neck through the window. He was a big guy, six two or three, and he was wearing a .45 in a shoulder rig, but no vest. He opened the refrigerator, took out a bottle of beer, and twisted off the cap before he closed the refrigerator door. Tony and Nicole crouched under the window waiting until they couldn't hear the truck anymore. They nodded to each other. Tony shouldered his AR-15 and stood up. Thick Neck was gone.

They moved around the back of the house and up the other side past two darkened bedrooms, which brought them back to the front. They peeked in the living room window. Thick Neck faced the TV with a remote control in his right hand and his beer in his left. Tony clicked his rifle to full auto, sprang up in front of the window, and sprayed the room with bullets. The rifle wailed like a high-speed jackhammer. The window shattered inward. Thick Neck jerked around like a dancing marionette. When he finally fell, Tony stopped firing.

Nicole ran in through the front door. "Overkill, don't you think?"

Tony was right behind her. Thick Neck was lying in a pool of blood, his chest and legs riddled with bullets, the broken neck of the beer bottle still in his hand. Tony checked his throat for a pulse. "Dead."

They turned on the lights in the bedrooms. In the first bedroom were four cots, cases containing rifles, and four packed carry-on bags. In the second bedroom, a military laptop computer sat on a folding table. Next to it was a small safe. "Bingo," Tony said. He glanced at Nicole. "Watch the front."

He gave the safe a push. It was bolted down. He squatted in front of it. Old-style dial combination. Guess they didn't want to risk someone using a magnet on an electronic keypad. He rubbed his hands together. It was always a pleasure to open one of these old boxes. He rotated the dial, listened for the clicks, and worked out the combination on a scrap of paper. Success. He turned the handle. The bolt slid back into the door. Now for the hard part. He cracked the door open just so the front edge of the door cleared the face of the safe. No wire visible. He opened it a little more. Still no wire. On the third go-around, he spotted the thin steel booby trap wire. He glanced around the top of the table, looked in a backpack lying on the floor, but he didn't see any wire cutters.

He went into the living room, where Nicole was standing in the dark looking out the window. "We need some wire cutters."

They went into the kitchen and looked through the drawers. Mismatched silverware, cooking utensils, old pots and pans, but no wire cutters. They went back into the living room and turned on the lights. No wire cutters lying about anywhere. They went into the bedroom and went through the luggage. Nothing. They went back into the living room. "There have to be wire cutters," Tony said.

"Maybe one of the other guys has them," Nicole replied.

"Or maybe this guy." Tony knelt beside Thick Neck and went through his pockets. In his front right pocket with his change and a container of Tic Tacs was a multitool with a wire cutter in it.

He went back to the safe, cut the wire, and then continued to open the door in stages while he looked for other wires. Finally, he pushed the door open with a wooden kitchen spoon while he stood to one side. The cut wire went to a triggering device on a box with a hole in the front.

"What is it?" Nicole asked.

"Never seen anything like this before. And I'm not going to touch it." He pulled the blackmail envelope, a stack of cash, and a 9 mm pistol out of the safe. The envelope had been opened. He looked at the paper inside. The printed text was in a code, with a hand-written decryption written in underneath. The decryption looked like a numbered bank account and a password. Jackpot. So this was what was worth killing for. He put the paper back in the envelope. He handed the envelope and the money to Nicole, shut the safe door, and put the pistol into his pocket.

"Let's get out of here."

In the meantime, Missy left Lysistrata and drove six blocks to Diamond Jack's, a neighborhood bar with pool tables and pinball machines. She needed to be sure she wasn't being followed. Robertson was pushing her, which was not like him. He might know she was being followed and he might not. That was the problem. Not only didn't she know if she could trust him, she didn't know if he really knew what was going on.

Diamond Jack's was as empty as you would expect on a Sunday night. A couple was playing pool. Two guys sat at the bar playing cribbage and nursing beers. Another guy was watching a basketball game on TV and talking with the bartender. Missy took a barstool close to the back and ordered a beer. She waited thirty minutes. Then she called a rideshare, laid some money on the bar, and went to the ladies' room, where she opened the window and climbed out into the alley. That was why she'd chosen this bar. Working window and a short drop to the ground.

She went down the alley, came out on the next street, and walked two blocks to Katie's Apparel. A Camry was just pulling up. She got in the back.

"You're going to the Three Pines Motel on Beech Street?" the driver asked.

"Yes."

A hooded man wearing dark clothes watched Missy from the shadows at the entry to the alley. Just as she got into the Camry, a truck pulled up beside him. He climbed in. "That's the one," the hooded man said.

"Got you," the driver replied.

They took off after the car. The hooded man got out his phone. "Major? She's on the move."

. . .

FRENCH DROVE down the gravel road to the farmhouse. The passports were beautiful. Real art. They had the bank-account numbers and the passcodes. Just as soon as they dealt with the safecracker, they'd be on a plane to Switzerland. Split the money into separate accounts. Handshakes all around. Never see any of them again. Setting up the corporation last year and buying the house in New Zealand had been a genius move. No one would be able to find him.

Where was the farmhouse? He peered into the dark. Why were the lights off? He pulled into the front yard so that his headlights shined through the living room. Broken windows. Where was Rollings? He pushed the truck door open and dropped to the ground behind it. He pulled his pistol. He crawled across the patchy grass to the front window and peeked in. In the light from the headlights, he saw Rollings lying on the floor. *Damn it.*

He pushed the front door open, stepped into the shadows in the living room, and worked his way through the dark house until he came back to the living room from the kitchen. The place was empty. He flipped on the wall switch. Blood, bullet holes, and broken glass. He walked back through the house, turning on the lights as he went. Their luggage had been tossed. Rollings dead, the house searched. Who could have done it? He went to the safe. The wire had been cut. The envelope and the money were gone. This wasn't bad luck. This was the safecracker. He pulled out his phone. "Rick? Rollings is dead. Collect Missy and the girl. Bring them here."

He paced through the house, walking from room to room, getting angrier with each step. Robertson was dependable. He was in this up to his eyeballs. Which meant that Missy was the weak link. She'd sold them out. He snatched up a kitchen chair and beat it against the wall until it was in pieces. They had to know everything she knew, and they had to know before she died. They were getting the bank-account numbers back. They were killing the safecracker. They were going to be on the plane in the morning. He tossed the last piece of the chair into the living room. Get a grip. Now was not the time for emotion. He called Robertson.

"Paul? Rollings is dead. The numbers are gone. Rick and Gary are collecting Missy and her girlfriend."

"Take it easy," Robertson said. "She belongs to me."

"I don't care."

"She'll tell us whatever she knows."

"You can bet on that."

"Wait for me before you start."

TONY AND NICOLE were back at their motel room. They had the account numbers, $25,000 in cash, plus the $5,000 and the diamonds. Tony sat on the bed and leaned back against the headboard. "This job is beginning to pay for itself."

Nicole kicked off her shoes. "Do you want a glass of wine?"

"Please." He got out his phone to call Missy. The phone rang four times. He thought it was going to voice mail when she finally picked up.

"Better be good," Missy said.

"You sound out of breath. Am I interrupting something?"

"Talk fast."

"Plan worked. I got the package and narrowed the odds."

"By how many?"

"One."

"That's not enough."

"It's a start."

"You know they're coming to kill you."

"This is my worried voice."

"Ha ha." She ended the call.

Nicole handed him a glass of wine.

"Thanks." He sipped his wine and stared off at the door to the motel room.

"What's up?" she asked.

"Tomorrow morning, we're moving to a new motel. French is going to be pissed off when he gets back to the farmhouse."

"What are we going to do with the account numbers?"

"Garcia wants them, but that doesn't mean she's going to get them. We've got what looks like the complete info for a numbered account. Ill-gotten gains for sure. If we knew which bank, we could walk in and take whatever's in the account. No questions asked. This could be the score of a lifetime. I'm not just giving it up because a Fed wants it."

At the Three Pines Motel, Missy and Betty were cuddled together in the dark in the bed closest to the bathroom. "Who was that?" Betty asked.

"The guy I've been helping. He just ripped off the bad guys. They're going to be after him hard now."

"How much longer until we can go home?"

"I'm amazed he's lasted this long."

Betty sighed. "Oh girl, I've missed you so much."

"Me too. I've been cashing in favors, sleeping on couches. To be lying here with you—even in this place—it's heaven. When this is all done, let's go on a spa vacation."

"Massages and beauty treatments?"

"The complete pamper package. Private balcony, fine dining— we're going to get spa'd out."

The door to the motel room slammed open against the wall, the doorjamb shattering where the bolt had been locked. Two men in dark clothes and masks rushed in. Betty screamed. Missy snatched up her phone, grabbed Betty by the arm, pulled her into the bathroom, and locked the door. They were naked. There was no window. There was nothing to use as a weapon. "Get in the tub," Missy said. She speed-dialed Tony.

8

GETTING EVEN

Tony's smartphone rang. He picked it up from the bedside table and glanced at the screen. Missy. What could she want? "Yeah?"

"They found me!"

The line went dead.

He turned to Nicole. "The mercs just scooped up Missy."

"Shit. What's our play?"

"I don't owe her anything. But she's going to break and put the mercs on me. I don't know what she knows. Not for sure. And if they're all together, it might be the best opportunity to finish them off."

"So we're back to tailing Robertson?"

"Yes."

Nicole scooted off the edge of the bed and picked up her pants from the floor.

Tony pulled Robertson's signal up on the tracker app on his phone. "Looks like he's going back to the farmhouse."

"That place is a mess."

"It'll scare the hell out of Missy and they'll only have one place to burn, so it's pretty much a win-win if they can stay on a tight time line."

"We're gearing up?"

"Kevlar, assault rifles, and sidearms. Extra ammo. If everyone's there, there'll be French, Robertson, and the two mercs. French has got to go."

Nicole drove the Camry. Tony watched Robertson's movements on the tracker app. Nicole flipped off the headlights just before she turned onto the gravel road. They knew where they were going, but the night seemed horror-movie dark. She rolled into the grass and up to the fence in the same place they had parked the first time. Every window in the farmhouse was lit up. Robertson's Explorer was parked out front. The mercs could be anywhere. Tony turned off the Camry's inside lights before they opened the car doors. There was no room for error this time. They put on the Kevlar, checked their weapons, and put on the communication headsets. Then they moved silently across the road, Tony about six feet ahead and to Nicole's left. Tony was carrying his AR-15, Nicole was carrying the sniper rifle. As they approached the house, she moved off into the dark.

Tony crawled up under the kitchen window and peeked in. Missy and another woman, wearing bathrobes, were duct-taped into kitchen chairs. The other woman, a thin Eurasian with bad bedhead, was sobbing. The girlfriend. So Missy had been telling the truth, at least about that. French and Robertson were standing over Missy. A merc was leaning against the sink, leering at the girlfriend. In his mind, he was already on top of her. Tony crawled away from the window. He clicked on his comms. "We're missing one merc," he whispered.

"Affirmative. If he's out here, I haven't found him yet."

Tony crawled away from the house and took out the Garcia cell phone. It rang twice before she picked up.

"It's about time," Garcia said.

"I'm getting ready to clean up your mess. You keep the cops away, and maybe you'll find your paperwork in the rubble."

"Where are you?"

"Please, you've been tracking this phone from the first minute."

"I want Robertson."

"We'll see how it works out." Tony ended the call.

He crawled back to the kitchen window. He could hear French speaking: "You're going to tell us where he is."

"All I have is a phone number," Missy said.

Tony heard a smack.

French continued. "Do you want us to hurt your girl?"

"No. No. But I don't know anything else. I'm telling you the truth."

ROBERTSON'S PHONE RANG. He glanced at the face of the phone and then answered it. "Yeah?"

"I know you know I'm on to you," Garcia said. "Get out of there if you want to live."

He slid his phone back into his pocket. If he left, Missy and her girlfriend were dead. It didn't matter what French told him. But Garcia wouldn't lie to him. Really, at this point, he couldn't even be sure that French wasn't planning to murder him too. He'd talked himself into this spot step by step, always agreeing to go along. To save his marriage. To bolster his retirement. But then the killings had started. The Chens and Clemens. He was in too deep. Now Garcia was going to squeeze him. He'd be lucky to stay out of prison. But at least he wouldn't die here today. Missy knew the risks. She'd been well paid all along, and the girlfriend? She wasn't his responsibility. "I have to go."

"What do you mean?" French asked.

"Supervisor wants me."

"At one o'clock in the morning?"

"Which means I've got to go."

"You can't leave," Missy said. "You promised me you'd take care of us."

"And I will." He turned to French. "Wait for me. I'll be back in an hour."

"How about if we finish this first?"

"Do you want my supervisor hunting for me?"

"Okay, we'll wait. Get out of here."

TONY HEARD the front door slam and a car start. Nicole spoke over the comms. "That was Robertson. There's three trucks out back, the dead guy's and two others."

"Got you."

From in the kitchen, French said, "Paul can be a little squeamish. He's never really been a field agent. Now it's just us party animals. Option one: You tell us everything you know about the safecracker. Option two: We make you watch while we mess up your girl, and then you tell us everything you know about the safecracker."

"Are you going to let us go?"

"Missy. You're a friend of Paul's. You're a professional criminal. I know you can't rat us out. I'd love to have Gary drive you back to the motel. What's the safecracker's name?"

"He doesn't have a name, as far as I know. He has a new name every time I see him. People in the game call him the Traveling Man. Never heard anyone call him anything else."

"Where's he staying?"

"He's been to three motels that I know of. God knows where he is now. Another motel, I guess."

"You have to do better than that."

Her voice broke. "If I knew where he was, I'd tell you. He's nothing to me. If he knew you had me, he'd be as quick to kill me as you. Paul and me go way back."

"All that's just fine, but it doesn't do me any good. Gary? Help the girlfriend out of her robe."

Tony tapped his comms on. He whispered, "When you get a shot, take it."

"Got you," Nicole replied.

Through the sniper scope, she watched Gary cross over to Betty with a kitchen knife in his hand, cut through the duct tape on her wrists, and pull her to her feet. She tried to push him away. He smacked her face. When he grabbed the lapels of her robe, Nicole fired. The window above Tony's head shattered, shards of glass flying into the room. Nicole fired again. The first slug hit Gary in the abdomen. He lurched sideways. The second shot spun him around. Betty screamed, clutched herself, and started jumping around. French dove for the floor and started crawling toward the back bedroom. Missy struggled in her chair, bouncing it off the floor. "Get down, Betty, get down!" she yelled.

"No shot," Nicole said.

Tony lifted his assault rifle to his shoulder as he sprang up at the window. He put a row of slugs into French's back. French stopped crawling. A shot splintered wood from the window frame by Tony's head. He dropped to the ground. "Missy!" he yelled. "Sniper in back!"

Tony heard Nicole's voice over the comms. "I was on the move. Saw a flash. Can you draw him out?"

"I think I might have pulled a stitch, but I can run a few feet. I'm going to try for the closest truck."

Tony ran around the corner into the backyard. The only light was behind him, making him an obvious target. A shot came in to his right. He shifted left two steps. A shot came in to his left just as he shifted right again. He lunged, his rifle out in front of him. A shot came in over his head as he hit the ground behind the truck. Pain exploded from the stitches in his side. He saw stars. Just then, another shot rang out.

"Stay put," Nicole said. "If he comes to you, he's leaking. I'm sure of it."

Tony leaned back against the wheel of the truck. "Missy!" he yelled.

"Yeah?"

"Turn off the kitchen lights and stay put until you hear the all clear."

The backyard went dark. Tony crawled under the truck and watched the farm field in back of the house. He couldn't see or hear anything. The stars were bright, but not bright enough to light up the field. He slowed his breathing and kept scanning the distance.

In a thicket off to his right—was a branch moving? He shifted his rifle.

"Tony," Nicole said. "I got him. I'm coming in from your right."

He saw her appear out of the dark, carrying two rifles. He crawled out from under the truck, sat on the bumper, and waited on her. "Good shooting."

"Thanks. How's your wound?"

"Sore, but I don't think it's bleeding." He stood up. "Missy!" he yelled. "We're coming in!"

The kitchen lights switched on. Missy stood in the doorway holding French's pistol. She looked at Nicole. "I was wondering when you'd turn up."

French and Gary were lying where they had fallen. Betty was sitting in a corner, head down, her arms wrapped around her legs. Tony squatted over Gary, turned out his pockets, and then moved on to French.

"Find anything?" Nicole asked.

"Phones, car keys, fake passports, hotel keycard, and a card from the downtown Hilton. Passports look pretty good."

Missy tucked French's pistol into the pocket of her robe and helped Betty to her feet. "How did you get Paul to leave?"

"I've got my ways."

"You knew French and his guy would fuck us up."

"I knew we could definitely kill two of them. Besides, you were playing both ends against the middle," Tony said.

"You would have done the same," Missy replied.

"Not to a partner."

She had her hand on the butt of her pistol. "I already told you I never meant for you or your guys to get hurt. That's on this bastard." She pushed at French with her foot.

"You got in over your head relying on Robertson. I get that. But that's all over now," Tony said.

Nicole handed Missy a set of car keys. "These should go to one of the trucks out back."

"You're going to let us go?"

Tony nodded. "You planted the transmitter, took your chances. That's got to mean something."

"What are you going to do about this mess?"

Tony surveyed the room. Two bodies, blood and spent bullets, fingerprints everywhere. And that was just the kitchen. "Burn it."

"Good luck," Missy said. "Don't bother to look for us. We're leaving town." Missy had her arm around Betty as they left through the back door.

Tony and Nicole watched them get into the second truck. "We've got to move fast," Nicole said.

Tony nodded. "Garcia probably didn't call the cops, but you never can tell."

"We didn't bring any gasoline."

"What about the stove? It's gas."

"Build a fire in a living room and break the gas line?"

"That should do it."

"What about the guy in the yard?"

"Not our fingerprints."

Nicole dragged the stove away from the wall. Tony pulled a carry-on bag from the front bedroom into the living room, where he opened the bag and flipped the clothes into a loose pile. Nicole brought him a piece of cardboard she'd lit at the stove. He held it to the piled-up clothing. The fire sputtered and caught hold. He stood in the living room where he could see Nicole in the kitchen and watched the fire until the flames licked up sides of the carry-on bag. The smoke smelled poisonous. "Do it!" he yelled.

Nicole smashed the gas line fitting at the back of the stove with her rifle butt. Gas hissed out into the kitchen, filling the room with its rotten egg smell. They trotted out the front door and down the road to their car. They put their heavy gear in the trunk and turned the car around to leave. Then they sat in the dark and watched the house. The flames were bright through the broken windows.

"You sure that's all of them?" Nicole asked.

"Yeah. Four of them, plus French."

"Feel better about Duke and Barker?"

"Not really."

"We going to the Hilton?"

"There's nobody to stop us. Why skip dessert?"

The explosion rocked the car. Bits of roofing, glass, and charred wood rained down around them. The farmhouse was an inferno.

"That took longer than I thought it would," Tony said.

Nicole turned on the headlights, and they drove away.

MEANWHILE, Garcia and Robertson sat in a government sedan on the street across from the downtown Hilton. There were no pedestrians on the sidewalks, and only the occasional car drove by. Garcia opened a laptop, pulled up a video, and passed the laptop to Robertson. "This is the first video of you and the perps—this is last year in Kyrgyzstan. Go ahead and flip through them. Either you're working undercover for the task force, in which case you write up everything you know, get a commendation, and retire at full pension. Or you're a criminal, you tell everything as part of your plea deal, you lose your pension, and you go to prison. Either way works for me."

Robertson closed the laptop. "I just needed more retirement money."

"Don't we all."

He looked out the window into the dark. "I'm working for the task force."

"Congratulations."

"I still don't have enough money."

"Jesus, Paul. Do what everyone else does. J&R is always looking for consultants. Eight to five, no nights, no weekends. Everybody tells me it's like getting free money. And you won't be bothering your wife in the middle of the day."

He passed the laptop back to her. "You haven't asked me for the envelope."

"Because you don't have it."

He put his hand on the door handle.

"Tomorrow morning, bright and early. And Paul, I know it looks bleak right now, but don't go to a motel and kill yourself. It would be a waste."

He got out of the sedan. She watched him in her rearview mirror until she saw her operative start following him. Then she sat there, watching the front of the hotel, until she saw the con man and his old partner, dressed like business travelers, no luggage, walk through the heavy glass doors.

TONY AND NICOLE strolled through the front door of the Hilton, past the sofas and potted plants, past the registration desk, and to the elevators, arm and arm, as if they'd had a very satisfying dinner followed by a number of drinks. There was no one else waiting. On the twelfth floor, they got off and walked down the empty hallway lined with the occasional Do Not Disturb sign hanging from a door or room service tray of dirty dishes sitting on the carpet. The keycard still worked. But the room was empty and clean. Nothing in the closet or the bathroom or the dresser drawers or the room safe or under the bed. They were ready to leave when there was a knock on the door. Tony pulled his Glock. "Into the closet," he whispered.

Nicole stepped into the dark side of the closet. Tony kept his pistol behind the door as he opened it. He smiled his most charming smile. "Agent Garcia."

She was carrying a shoulder bag. An automatic pistol was holstered on her hip. "You can put your gun away."

"Please come in."

He opened the door and holstered his Glock.

Garcia closed the door and leaned back against it. "Your partner can come out."

Nicole stepped out of the closet.

"What can we do for you?" Tony asked.

"The envelope that contains the bank-account numbers. Don't bother to act like you don't have it. I'm sure you can be very convincing. Just hand it over."

"What about our deal?"

"You broke our deal."

"I was going to bring it to you tomorrow."

"I'm losing my patience. You give me the envelope, or you're going to jail."

"No, you don't want this sad incident on the internet or in the papers. You keep the deal, and we keep quiet. It's a win-win."

"You won't be telling your story to anyone from a black site."

"We've created a video. It's all set to go out on the internet if we don't stop it. Wide broadcast. You'll never take it down."

"You're bluffing."

"Do you want to find out? Wouldn't it be easier just to play nice and take the win? You'll have your bad player and the accounts. What more could you ask for?"

She went to the desk by the window, took her laptop out of her bag, clicked on her secure browser, went into the FBI's site, input her clearance password, and pulled up the case file. "Does this look familiar?"

Tony read the page. Little Jimmy. The Crazy Devils. El Paso and Ciudad Juarez. "That's the case. Close it up."

"The envelope."

He handed her the envelope. She read over the encryption and the translation. "That's Clemens's handwriting, all right."

"I sent you the photo of him at the airport. They got him to do the decryption, and then they murdered him."

She folded the paper into the envelope and put it into her pocket.

"Do your thing," he said.

She input a few sentences, added her name and ID number, and pressed the return. "Take that one off your list. No big deal. The FBI has still got plenty of reasons to hunt you."

"But that case is closed. The physical evidence goes into deep storage."

"Yeah." She logged out and put away her laptop. "I don't want to see you again. You won't get another pass from me."

He smiled. "Almost forgot. Here's something extra." He handed her the passports. "Just in case you start to think your boy Robertson was an innocent bystander."

They gave Garcia enough time to get on the elevator before they started down the hall to the stairwell. They walked down into the basement parking garage and came out of the garage onto a side street. The attendant in the office didn't notice them. There was no one suspicious standing on the street or sitting in a parked car. They walked away from the Hilton.

"Why did you care so much about the El Paso job?" Nicole asked.

"The Crazy Devils never found out we double-crossed them. But the FBI would have known. It had to be in the evidence. Little Jimmy and his guys are locked up, but their business is still going, and the dirty cops are still being paid."

"And now those files are buried."

"Federal warehouse. Dirty cops can't get to them."

"So that was the bonus."

Tony eyed the row of cars parked along the street. "We should dump the Camry."

"How about that Audi?" she asked.

He popped the door locks and hotwired the car. "Somebody told me they were going to make these cars harder to steal."

"Who?"

"Can't remember. Somebody who didn't know what they were talking about."

He drove over three blocks and double-parked in the street next to the Camry. They moved their gear into the trunk of the Audi. "Wipe it or burn it?" Nicole asked.

"Let's be extra careful."

THE NEXT DAY, Tony and Nicole sat at a table in a bar at the airport. They were both leaving Mitchellville, going in different directions. Nicole would eventually end up in San Francisco; Tony wasn't sure where he would land yet. "Five grand plus the diamonds and twenty-five grand out of the safe. Not too shabby," he said.

"Plane fare, gear purchase, visit to the vet, two guys dead."

"True enough. But we sold the gear back, and there're no loose ends."

"Except for Garcia and Robertson and Missy and her girl."

"Garcia we're stuck with. Missy and her girl I don't think we have to worry about. Robertson is on my to-do list."

"Isn't he under Garcia's protection?"

"Don't care. He's a crook. He's in the game, and he set me up to be murdered. Once he's gone, she won't be able to dig into it without exposing the rotten mess he was part of."

"She'll still come after you."

"Maybe, but her honesty is her limitation." He shifted his head to watch a man pulling a wheeled suitcase.

"Someone we know?"

"No. Looked a little like Buddy for a minute."

"That would be surprising."

"It would be." He squeezed her hand. "It's great to see you."

"It's great to see you. But have you learned your lesson?"

"Which one?"

"Going off half-cocked. I'm beginning to think you've had one concussion too many."

He held up his right hand like he was taking an oath. "It's back to basics for me, baby. When I deal with Robertson, I'm going to scout it out, take my time, plan out every detail, and double up on the escape routes. I don't care how long it takes."

"Now you're talking. Give me a call when it's set."

"Maybe. You going to find a way to settle down when you're with Denison?"

"It's so boring, Tony. Coming out here to help you, doing our thing, even for a few days—God, I miss it. The straight life is so empty: Nothing to think about, nothing to do. I just don't know if I'm up for it long term. I'm actually looking forward to dealing with Lily's little problem."

"You should just cut her loose."

"Please. This little project will be a walk in the park. With the info

Kevin provided, we've got this asshole's whole life. He'll be begging for mercy in short order."

"If you've got the right guy."

"We've got him."

"And then you'll have to settle down, protect your cover like you're setting up a scam."

She pulled the straw from her rum and Coke and set it on the napkin. "Tell me, honestly: Could you do it?"

"The straight life? If I had enough money, and it was just me and you—some tropical paradise—yeah, I think maybe I could."

"But now you're off to Chicago."

"Layover. Remember that woman I met online last year? The one in Iowa?"

"Vaguely."

"I'm hoping to reconnect with her. I dropped the ball while I was here, and it's been a little while, but she seemed pretty needy. So if she texts me back, I'm going straight to the cold call."

"What's your story?"

"With her, I'm C.D. Abbot, semi-retired security consultant, so I'm going to say I was out of the country on a super-secret government contract. It just came up. I couldn't get in touch with anyone."

"You'll sell her."

"If she doesn't have a man, I'm betting I'll be moving in. Otherwise, I think I'm going to get lost in Miami for a few weeks."

Nicole glanced at the clock on her phone. "I need to go to my gate."

"Always thinking of you."

"Always thinking of *you.*"

"Call me before you need me."

"You too." She gave him a quick kiss, and she was gone.

9

BACK IN THE BAY

Nicole yo-yoed back and forth across the country, making sure she wasn't being followed, spent the night at John F. Kennedy International Airport in New York City, and finally took a direct flight to San Francisco. She was exhausted. She caught a cab outside of baggage claim and rode into the city to Denison's condo. No one was home. She texted Denison, took a shower, read his reply—*Home in two hours. Love you*—and went to bed.

She heard him open the bedroom door to peek into the darkened room. "Hey, Jimmy. I'm awake," she said.

He sat down on the bed beside her. "You look fine."

"Yeah. There was nothing to it. Tony needed my help. I got him to the doctor, nursed him until he got his strength back."

"Before you left, I think maybe I overreacted."

"No, James, you were right. I shouldn't have been taking chances just to catch a thrill. Never again. I promise."

"What should we do about Lily?"

"We're not going to do anything. I'm going to take care of it."

"How?"

"You don't want to know."

"But no taking chances?"

"No taking chances."

"Then how are you going to—"

"Jimmy. Just relax. This isn't Cricket Bay."

THAT EVENING, Nicole and Lily sat on stools at the kitchen island sipping white wine. Nicole had made the room off limits to Denison while they discussed their plans. "So," Nicole asked, "where do we stand?"

"Nothing's changed. He's got my driver's license, my phone, and my wallet. He knows where I live. I may just be paranoid, but I thought someone was following me on Sunday. I tried to call you."

"Sunday was crazy. But like I told you, we've got all the info we need." Nicole opened an accordion folder and pulled out a stack of papers paper-clipped into sections. "Copies of driver's licenses are on top."

Lily flipped through the sections. She stopped at a driver's license photo of a man with a shaved head and a droopy mustache and pulled it out of the pile. "That's him."

"You sure?"

She nodded. "Definitely." She passed that section to Nicole.

"Your guy is Fred Sanders." Nicole pulled the paper clip and glanced through the individual sheets. "We've got his insurance info, home address, work address, plus info off his computers and his smartphone."

"All that?"

Nicole nodded.

"What do we need his computer info for?"

"Looking for something to trade. Hoping for some sick porn, but no luck. Looks like he's a family man, wife and two kids—I'm guessing the daughter is fifteen—who's out horndogging after young women."

"Already knew he was a lech."

"Daughter's a pretty little thing who looks a little like you."

"So he's fucked up. What are we going to do about him?"

"We're going to take pictures of him being a bad boy. Then we're going to send him those pictures, with the promise that his wife and kids and work will see them if he doesn't give you your stuff and get lost."

"You've done this before?"

"Many times."

"And it always works?"

"Oh yeah. Not only will it work, but after you have your handbag back, we're going to blackmail him until we get back our out-of-pocket expenses."

"I don't know, Nicole. I'd be happy if he'd just leave me alone."

"I thought you liked the thrill of the game."

"This stopped being fun a long time ago."

She patted Lily's hand. "Don't worry. We'll have this turned around before you know it."

"But how? How do you know how to do this kind of thing? Hackers and blackmail—even joyriding cars. I googled Denison. He's a rich guy. This is a rich guy's house. You wear nice clothes, don't have a job. You're a rich guy's girlfriend. It just doesn't make sense."

"I've told you before, Lily, I'm not going to explain myself to you. What's your best option right now? You won't sleep with Sanders. You won't have him beat down. You won't leave town. So you've got to push back."

"When you put it like that, it seems so obvious. It's just—I don't know. I don't want to get into more trouble. I want to get out."

"Call the police."

"No way. There's two of them. I can't win a he-said she-said."

"Then this is how you do it."

"But what's James going to think of all this?"

"He's not going to know. Nobody's going to know. That's the whole point."

Lily looked off across the room, a vacant expression on her face.

"What's it going to be?" Nicole asked.

Lily sighed. "Okay, you're right. This is my best option. What do we do next?"

"We're going to start following Sanders after work."

The next afternoon, Nicole and Lily were sitting in a stolen Prius across the street from ACS Associates, an accounting firm located in a new high-rise out in the suburb of Ferndale. Lily was wearing a straw hat and sunglasses, Nicole a blonde wig and dark makeup. "Are you sure we won't get caught?" Lily asked.

"Person comes out to their parking spot after work. Their car is gone. They look around, start questioning their memory. Eventually, they call the cops. They make a report. Now it's an hour later. They go home, cursing their bad luck. The police report filters into the system. Now it's tomorrow. See how this works?"

"So no one's looking for this car yet."

"The owner hasn't even finished work yet. Relax."

At 5:00 p.m., cars began to empty out of the parking deck. "Keep an eye out," Nicole said.

"There he is." A pudgy man with a shaved head and a sad mustache drove out onto the street in a blue BMW.

"That the guy?" Nicole asked.

"Yeah."

"And the car?"

"Definitely."

"So you were macking on *that* guy in a bar?"

"Yeah."

"And he overpowered you in the parking lot?"

"There were two of them. And nobody ever hit me before."

"I'd forgotten about that. Just another reason to straighten him out."

They followed Sanders through the rush-hour traffic south into the residential suburbs. He pulled into a driveway on Ponderosa Avenue. The house was a renovated two-story built after World War II. White with brown trim. The brick steps led up to a small porch. The wooden front door had a round window in it. Nicole checked the address against the information they had. It was his home address. Lily drove around the block and pulled into a spot on the street with a good view of the front. Twenty minutes later, a twelve-year-old boy, tall and thin, his backpack hanging from his shoulder and track cleats in one hand, went up the steps and into the house.

"Does Sanders go out after dinner?" Nicole asked. "Or is he in for the evening when he comes home? Today is Wednesday. He met you on a Tuesday. Was his wife out of town? Was he entertaining a client, or does he often go out on a weekday night? See how I'm thinking? We're going to have to stay on him if we're going to put him in play at the first opportunity."

Lily nodded.

"Good. I'm going home."

"What?"

"I'm meeting James for dinner. This is your mess, girlfriend. You stay here until ten, or you call me and follow him if he leaves."

"What do I do with the car?"

"I'd take it back. Keep the hat and sunglasses on while you're in the parking deck. Catch a cab a couple of blocks over. Or just leave it somewhere. It's up to you."

Nicole walked away from Sanders's house to the next major intersection and ordered a rideshare. When she got back to the condo, she took off the wig before she got out of the car and pushed it inside her jacket. She found Denison in the living room.

"Hey, honey," she said.

Denison looked up from his iPad. A glass of red wine sat on the table beside him. "What's with the makeup?" he asked.

"Working on Lily's problem. Did you see my text?"

"Yes."

"The Vietnamese should be here in just a few minutes."

"I can't wait. I'm starving. The bottle's on the counter."

She went back into their bedroom, dropped her handbag on the bed, and went into the bathroom to clean the makeup off her face. She came back into the living room with a glass of wine in her hand.

"There she is," he said.

She sat on the arm of his chair, leaned down, and kissed him. "Busy day?"

"We're still getting static from the neighbors about our new building. Everybody's in favor of helping the homeless unless the building's on their street."

"That's a drag."

"We'll get the permits. It's just going to take longer than we want." He sipped his wine. "What about you?"

"Don't want to tell you about things you might need to deny. Let's just say I'm being very careful."

"Okay. You thought about the career counseling?"

"As soon as I have the time."

The doorbell rang.

"Finally," Nicole said. "It must be the food."

On Thursday, it was more of the same. Sanders drove home, and Lily sat on the street in a new stolen car. But on Friday, Sanders walked out the front of the building with three men. "There's the other guy," Lily said. "The tall guy with the bad comb-over. I don't know the two young guys."

They got into a Lincoln MKT that was waiting at the curb. Nicole and Lily followed the Lincoln to the Cross Winds brewpub and pulled into a spot at the back of the parking lot. "What are we doing?" Lily asked.

"We're letting them settle. Then I'm going to do a walk-through to see what they're up to."

Twenty minutes later, Nicole pushed her way through the throng in the entry to the brewpub. Happy hour was in full swing. The horseshoe-shaped bar was crowded, and the tables were full. She moved through the space as if she were the latecomer to a party, scanning the faces as she went along. There they were in the corner, eating chicken wings and drinking beer. Comb-over had set his watch on the table next to his smartphone. One of the young guys finished speaking, and everyone laughed. Nicole turned into the women's restroom and washed her hands. They were going to be a while. She wove her way back through the crowd in the entry. The people waiting for tables seemed glad to see her, or anyone, leave.

"So?" Lily asked.

"They're here for supper."

"Is it worth waiting? The young guys don't look like they fit in."

"What do bad players look like? It's Friday night. Time for blowing off steam and misbehaving. We're going to wait them out. There's a Mexican place across the street. Go get us some takeout."

"Anything in particular?"

"Whatever you're having. And a Diet Coke."

Lily got out of the car. Nicole watched her cross the street. She felt the tingling in her back teeth that told her something was going to happen tonight. She hoped she was right. She got out her phone and called Denison. "Baby, it's me. How's your day?"

"For me, good. But I got an email from Bell. She's not happy. Skip's wife wants their daughter to be the flower girl, and Bell thinks she's too young."

"Well, maybe this will be the worst of it."

"I'm not holding my breath. Where are you?"

"I won't be home for dinner. I ordered you some food from that farm-to-table place you like. They should be delivering in about a half hour."

"You didn't have to do that."

"I know. I just wanted to make sure you got a good meal. You would have eaten those old leftovers out of the fridge."

"When will you get home?"

"I don't know. Hoping to clear up Lily's problem. Don't wait up."

"Be careful."

"It's my new name. Love you."

"Love you too."

An hour later, Nicole and Lily were still lounging in the car, takeout trash scattered around them, when Sanders and his friends came out of the brewpub and shook hands on the sidewalk. The two young guys went off in different directions. Sanders and Comb-over got into another rideshare, this time an Audi.

"They aren't driving," Lily said.

"Maybe they decided it wasn't worth the risk."

Nicole set her Diet Coke into a cupholder and put the car in gear. They followed the Audi out of the prosperous suburbs and into an old neighborhood surrounding a closed industrial plant. "I can't believe it," Lily said. "They're going back to Lucky Joe's."

The Audi let them out in front of the bar. A large man wearing a leather vest sat on a stool by the door. He nodded them in. Nicole pulled into a spot on the street. "This is not good for us," she said. "The parking lot is too open. We won't be able to take any video without being seen."

"So are we done for the night?"

"It's still early. Let's see what happens."

They sat in the car, watching people come and go from the bar, the county top forty blasting from the building. The parking lot was soon full. Cars were circling the block looking for a parking place. Nicole and Lily sat low in their seats to avoid being seen. "How long?" Lily asked.

"I'll do a walk-through in a little while."

"You know, I really don't get you. When we first met, I thought you were just like me, a little older maybe, but just a girl looking to trade conversation for some free drinks."

"Yeah."

"And then when we crashed the wedding and you dared me to take the car keys, I thought, 'Okay, walk on the wild side'—I mean, I've returned a dress after I've worn it to a party. I know how to take a dare. But that was like I was just caught up in the moment. I didn't give it a second thought."

"Sure."

"But then when I tried to do it on my own and those guys had me in the parking lot—I've never been so scared."

"It's always scary the first time."

"Exactly. That's what you would say. Because those guys wouldn't have had a chance with you. You would have owned them then just like you're planning to own them now. We're here on this stakeout, planning to screw them up. My hands are sweaty, I don't know if my deodorant will hold up, and you're as calm as always. You live in an expensive condo. You don't need the money. You could buy your own drinks. I can't figure you out. It's like you're a government agent or something."

"I'm glad for the vote of confidence. But Lily, this is nothing. These aren't criminal masterminds. They're just assholes who are used to treating women like trash. I'll be back in a minute."

The bouncer smiled when she approached the door. "Hey, girl, don't think I've seen you around here before."

"I just moved into town."

He opened the door for her. The band was set up in the back corner. The lead singer, a woman in a short dress and a cowgirl hat, was belting out a classic about lost love. Nicole couldn't quite remember the name of the song. She squeezed up to the bar, smiled at the guy to her right, a younger guy with his steady date, and ordered a vodka tonic. Sanders and Comb-over were down the bar near the band, chatting up two age-appropriate women wearing tight dresses and a lot of rings. The women were holding up their end of the conversation, but they weren't touching or making the fluttery eye contact that indicated real interest. It was all so sad and obvious. She went back out the door.

"Leaving so soon?" the bouncer said.

"Need to get some cigarettes."

She crossed the street and got back in the car. "Looks like the boys are going to strike out."

"It's almost eleven."

"It's still too early to quit."

A Ford Fusion pulled up in front of Lucky Joe's. Sanders and Comb-over came out of the bar and climbed in. Nicole and Lily followed the Ford deeper into the old city until they were in a broken-down neighborhood that sported the first few signs of redevelopment. The Ford stopped in front of The Lion's Den, a seedy bar across the street from a new coffee shop and an organic grocery. Today's Urban Hits were blasting out onto the street. Drug dealers stood out in the open on the nearest street corner. Nicole pulled to the curb across the street from the bar.

"This neighborhood is shit," Lily said.

"And there's no parking lot," Nicole said. She reached into her handbag and pulled out a Glock. "You ever use one of these?"

"Are you crazy?"

"It's very simple. It's all set to go. Point and pull the trigger."

"I don't want it."

"I'm going to leave you in the car."

"Leave me in the car? What are you going to do?"

"See if there's an alley."

"I'll go with you."

She shook her head. "We can't risk losing the car. I'm going to leave this gun on the seat. Lock the doors. Don't open them for any reason. This street is like an ad for a rape crisis center."

"What about you?"

"I've got another gun."

Nicole adjusted her blonde wig before she stepped out of the car. She sauntered across the street to the bar. The bouncer grinned through silver teeth. Sanders and Comb-over really were slumming it. A long bar ran down one side of the space, a double row of tables down the other side. The place was dark and loud and crowded with desperation and privilege. Every woman who was by herself appeared to be working or hoping to work. Some of them were too broken down to put on much of a show. They were hovering like vultures, waiting for the booze or the drugs to have their effect on their potential customers. She saw Sanders and Comb-over crowded up to the bar. She dug her hand into her bag to grip her Glock, meandered through to the back, and went out the door by the bathrooms. The alley was narrow and filthy. Boxes were stacked next to the full dumpster. Two ragged men huddled together at the corner watched her with animal interest.

"Hey, sugarpie," one of them said. "How about a little action on the house?"

She waited until they were almost on top of her, pulled her Glock, and shoved it into the first man's throat. "Touch me."

Their hands went up. The other guy said, "Whoa, lady, no disrespect."

They started backward. She moved with them, keeping the gun in the first man's throat until they reached the corner. "Find another alley."

"Yes, ma'am."

They scurried off to the right. She turned left and came out on the corner behind their car. Nothing had changed. Music blasted out of the front of The Lion's Den, and the corner boys were calmly alert. She climbed back into the car.

Lily looked at her expectantly.

"Not the best setup. Can't watch the front and back at the same time. And we stand out too much inside."

"Wait for another time?"

"No. Let me think." Nicole looked at the front of the bar, the bouncer, the dealers on the far corner. Her mind worked back through the bar, thinking about the men and the women, how they presented, where the bartender seemed to call home base, out the back, the alley around the dumpster. "Either they're going to snag a working girl, or they're going somewhere else." She spoke more to herself than to Lily. "Maybe she'll do them in the john." She was quiet for a moment. "I'm going back in. You're going to turn this car around, drive down the side street behind us, park where you can look down the alley. Lock the car doors. By ready to film. I'll call you when they move."

"You sure? What if they spot you?"

"Lily, they don't know who I am."

"What do we do if they go in the restroom?"

"I don't know."

Nicole sauntered back across the street into the bar. "I didn't even see you slip out," the bouncer said.

Nicole squeezed in at the end of the bar, flagged the bartender, and ordered a whiskey on the rocks. It was watery. She kept her head down and her arms in close, giving every signal that she wanted to be left alone. Sanders and Comb-over, halfway down the bar, were expansive and exuberant. They were tourists, they knew everyone knew it, and they saw no reason to hide. Nicole sipped her drink. The

man beside her—he looked like a blaxploitation movie star circa 1977
—offered to buy her a drink. She smiled but shook her head. Sanders
and Comb-over were visibly drunk. They ordered another round.
Comb-over stumbled back toward the men's room. A woman in a
tight yellow dress stood up from a table, pushed up her boobs, and
started after him. As they got to the restrooms, she put her arm
through his and led him into the ladies' room.

Nicole stood up. She turned to the blaxploitation star. "Can you
watch my place?"

He nodded.

She walked back to the restrooms, ignoring the looks of the men,
and pushed open the ladies' room door. There were two stalls. Comb-
over was leaning against the far wall. Yellow Dress was on her knees
in front of him. "You like to watch?" he asked.

"Just need to tinkle," Nicole said. She went into the nearest stall
and sat on the seat. So they've been here before. She waited a few
minutes and flushed. When she came out of the stall, Yellow Dress
was sitting on the sink looking vaguely bored, and Comb-over was
standing between her legs, pumping like an overloaded truck on a
steep hill. Nicole went back to her seat at the bar.

The blaxploitation star said, "You don't look like you belong here.
Not by yourself, anyway."

She smiled. "I'm a PI on an adultery case."

He glanced down the bar at Sanders.

"You're very observant," she said.

"Just playing the game of what doesn't belong," he replied.

"I'm not here to interrupt anybody's good time."

He nodded.

"How about if I buy *you* a drink?" she asked.

A few minutes later, Comb-over was back at the bar. He leaned
over and whispered to Sanders. They both laughed. Sanders turned
around and glanced over the single women sitting with Yellow Dress.
A skinny, dark-haired woman with a junkie's smile nodded. He
nodded back. She walked back to the restrooms with him, but they
ducked into the men's, not the ladies'.

The blaxploitation star smiled like he'd just heard a joke. "You going in there?"

Nicole reached into her handbag and placed a one-hundred-dollar bill on the bar next to her phone. "You get me the picture I need, the hundred is yours."

"Two hundred."

She brought out a second bill.

He picked up her phone and ambled back to the men's room.

Nicole watched Comb-over. He was in full-on drunk overconfidence mode, waving his hands around and talking to strangers. Two guys farther down the bar were also watching him, although they were trying hard not to be noticed. If Comb-over were by himself, he'd end the evening laid out in the alley. But Sanders came out of the men's room, zipped up his pants, and started back to his seat. The skinny woman was right behind him. Her hair looked wet. Sanders slapped Comb-over on the back. They spoke and laughed. A few minutes later, the blaxploitation star came out of the men's room and sauntered through the bar to his seat. He set the phone on the bar. Nicole looked at the photos. There was a video of Sanders getting a blow job. His face and the act were clear.

"Thanks," she said.

The blaxploitation star slid the $200 off the bar. "Easiest money I made today."

Nicole called Lily. "Pull around front."

The car was at the curb when she walked out of The Lion's Den. "Well?" Lily asked.

"I got the video."

Her mouth fell open. "How? How did you do that?"

"Got a guy to help me." She explained what had happened.

"So now we put the pressure on him?"

"This is the easy part. Let's dump this car and go home."

10

BLACKMAIL

The next morning, while Sanders was nursing a hangover in his home office, looking over a report on his laptop computer, his wife brought him an Ace Couriers delivery package. There was no return address. Inside was a thumb drive, a phone number, and a note printed on copy shop paper: *You give back the handbag, or this video goes to your wife and on the internet. How long to go viral with your name and workplace in the caption? Call after six.*

He held the thumb drive in his hand. Was this for real, or was it a computer virus? If it didn't mess up his computer right away, how would he know? The virus could be on a timer—maybe it wouldn't do anything for a week or a month. But it was obviously from Lily. What could be on this drive? How desperate was she? He slid the USB connector out of the drive body. He couldn't put this in his computer. That would be a dumb move. He needed to have Marty Colvin take a look at it. He was the head of security at ACS, and even though this problem was hard to explain, it was business-related. He'd been out with Kirby when she'd tried to steal his car. And keeping Kirby happy, and keeping his business, was job one. He got out his phone. "Marty, Fred here. I hate to bother you on the weekend, but I've got a problem. Can you meet me at the office?"

"What's it about?"

"I'd rather talk in person."

"That kind of problem? Okay, I'm at my kid's soccer game. How about I meet you in an hour?"

"Great. Let's meet in your office."

An hour later, they were in Colvin's office at ACS. Sanders explained the situation. Colvin leaned his bulk back in his chair and rubbed his bearded chin. "So you and Kirby go out alley-catting together."

"Ever since he got divorced. He's still going through his 'women are bloodsuckers' phase."

"Girl you were trying to pick up tried to steal your car."

"Yep."

"And you've been playing with her head."

"I know it sounds stupid when you say it like that."

"And now we have the mystery package."

"That's it. I was afraid to plug it into my computer."

Colvin reached into a desk drawer and pulled out a scuffed-up laptop. "This one is always air-gapped. We'll have a look at the thumb drive, and then I'll have IT scrub it on Monday."

He plugged the thumb drive into the laptop and opened the file. There was Sanders, roaring drunk, leaning against the wall in a filthy bathroom, with a woman, not his wife, on her knees between his legs. The lighting was bad, but it was obvious who he was and what was going on. "Jesus, Fred."

"Turn it off."

Colvin closed the file and pulled the thumb drive. "Is your career flashing before your eyes? Because it ought to be."

"I know. My job is gone if this gets out."

"That's the least of it."

"What do you mean?"

"Kirby's not in this video. His people see this, he denies any knowledge of such goings-on, we lose their business. The CEO would make sure that you never worked again."

"You really think so? I was doing this to keep Kirby happy."

"Are you kidding?"

"He wants to screw prostitutes. I just can't stand around. He'd be pissed. I've got to do what I've got to do to keep his business. Will you help me?"

Colvin pushed the thumb drive across the desk to Sanders. "Yeah, as long as we can keep this quiet, I'll help. But I'm not risking my job for you. Word gets out, it's all news to me."

"Thanks, Marty. I really appreciate it. How do you want to handle this?"

"You're making the six o'clock phone call from here."

At 6:00 P.M., Nicole and Lily were sitting at the kitchen island in Denison's condo waiting for the call from Sanders. "Do you think he's really going to call?" Lily asked.

"You saw the video. Do you think he wants his wife to see it?"

"Would we really send her a copy?"

"Never threaten what you won't do."

"But I don't want to ruin his life. I just want to be left alone."

"Take a deep breath. You didn't make his decisions for him. He did. He makes the right one now, he's home free."

The throwaway phone rang. Nicole put it on speaker.

"Who is this?" Sanders asked.

"You wanted to know what Lily has to trade. Now you know. You're starring in your own porno."

"How did you make that video?"

"You have sex in a restroom, what do you think is going to happen? You want to trade?"

"Yes. I want to trade."

"You give back the handbag and leave her alone, or we share the video."

"How do I know I can trust you?"

"Do you like your snowy-white reputation? Do you like being married? On your job, you meet with clients all day, how will that work if you're on the internet?"

"How do I know you won't post it after you get the handbag?"

"Can you take a chance? Let me predict the future. You've lost your job. Your kids won't look you in the eye."

"Let me think, for Christ's sake."

The line was quiet for a moment. Nicole and Lily exchanged a glance.

"Okay," Sanders said. "I'll give you the bag. Where do you want to meet?"

"We don't need to meet. FedEx it to her work. You know the address."

"And then we're good?"

"She gets her stuff back on Monday, and it's live and let live."

"Okay."

"On Monday. The clock is ticking."

Nicole ended the call.

"Wow," Lily said, "he's really going to do it."

"Maybe."

"Maybe?"

"This guy is a weasel. He's used to getting his way. He might think there's another way out."

"Like what?"

She shrugged. "Who knows? We'll see if he comes through on Monday. In the meantime, watch yourself."

SANDERS AND COLVIN were sitting in Colvin's office. "You did the right thing," Colvin said.

"But where does it end? That video has to be erased from wherever it's stored. Phone, computer, cloud."

"You know that's really not possible. There's no way to know if we've got the last copy."

"There's got to be a way to keep her quiet."

"She's turned the tables on you, got you by the short hairs. You've got to rely on her goodwill. Chances are she'll keep her word."

"That's not good enough."

"So what do you want to do? Beat her up? Kill her? I won't have anything to do with that."

Sanders threw up his hands. "God, no. I just need to know I'm safe."

"And there's not going to be another video?"

"Kirby's a massive client. If he wants to go out, I have to go out. But that rathole was by far the worst place he ever found."

"Okay," Colvin said. "This is as far as I'll go. We'll intimidate her. Scare her so bad she'll keep her mouth shut forever."

"How?"

"We'll use a contractor. He'll deal with her. That's the best way. Then nothing comes back on us."

"Will that work?"

"It's the best I can offer," Colvin said.

"Remember the good old days when client entertainment was just gambling and strip clubs? The biggest risk was a drunk driving charge."

"Seems like so long ago now."

MONDAY AFTERNOON, Lily was at her desk on her computer, planning the itinerary for a monthlong sailing trip along the coast of Italy and Croatia, when a FedEx driver brought her a box. Inside was her handbag, her wallet, and her phone. She flipped through her wallet. Her driver's license, her credit cards, even her cash was there. She input the password on her phone. It all looked fine. She smiled to herself. Was this nightmare finally over? She called Nicole.

"It worked."

"Great. We'll give it a week, and then we'll move on to the next phase. Remember, no extracurricular activities."

"You must be kidding. I'm not flirting for drinks anymore. And I don't want that guy's money."

"You're going to pay the computer hacker yourself?"

"Yes. I'm done with this. No more."

"You sure?"

"Yes."

"All right. It's your call."

The afternoon flew by. Lily couldn't remember the last time she had felt so good. So when Chrissie asked her if she wanted to come to happy hour at the corner bar, she said she could go for a few minutes. Jason, their other workmate, went along as well. The place was busy with the after-work crowd, but just as they arrived, three suits picked up from a table in the window, and they sat down.

"Split a pitcher?" Jason asked.

Lily and Chrissie nodded. He left for the bar. "You're awfully chipper," Chrissie said.

"Got some good news I was hoping for," Lily said.

"Well?"

"It's not something I'm ready to share."

Chrissie rolled her eyes.

Jason returned with a pitcher of beer and three glasses.

"So what's his name?" Chrissie asked.

"New boyfriend?" Jason asked. "Back up and fill me in."

Lily waved at them dismissively. She put on her official voice. "Move along. Nothing to see here."

Jason handed her a glass of beer. "Hey, before I forget, Didi and I are going camping next weekend. I know I just asked you a few weeks ago, but could you water the plants and feed the cats?"

"Don't the cats get mad that you always take the dogs and leave them behind?" Lily asked.

"These are cat-cats, not dog-cats. No dogs is a vacation for them."

"You and Didi are always camping," Chrissie said. "Why?"

"Hiking the trails, waking up with the birds, the dogs love it—"

Chrissie cut in. "That sounds horrible. I mean, once or twice a year I could get, but every weekend?"

"Just add the word 'spa' at the end," Lily said, "and she'd be onboard."

"Camping and spa," Chrissie said. "Those two words aren't in the same dictionary."

"Is there anything you like about the outdoors?" Jason asked.

"Makes a great view out of the window."

Lily glanced at her watch. "I've got to go."

"So soon?" Chrissie asked.

"I don't want to miss my yoga class." She turned to Jason. "Give me the keys on Friday. I've got you covered. See you guys tomorrow."

She walked out onto the street. As she turned the corner, a man yelled after her. He was of medium build, bearded, with shaggy dark hair. "Lily," he said. "I'm glad I caught you."

"Who are you?"

"You need to give up that video and all the copies."

"I don't know what you're talking about."

"You're a very bad liar, Lily. You give up the video, we verify it's deleted from all your devices and the cloud, or we stay on you until we find something we can use."

He turned away. Lily watched him disappear into the crowd. She took a left and walked away from the yoga studio. Just when she thought she was safe. What did he mean by "verify it's deleted"? A copy of a digital video is the same as the original. And even if there were some sort of tag or marker on the original, she could make a hundred copies and claim they didn't exist. Did they want access to all her devices and storage backups? How could they know she didn't have an extra thumb drive? Were they already hacking her life? Were they doing to her what she'd done to Sanders? Maybe she was going to have to run. Start all over somewhere else. Over a stupid little game. Her whole life upended over a joyride gone wrong. Tears welled up in her eyes. She took out her phone and speed-dialed Nicole.

"I have to see you."

"Is there a problem?"

"Yes."

"You're on the phone you lost."

"Yes."

"Don't say my name. The place we met—not the first time, not the second time, the third time. You know where I mean? Don't say it."

"I know."

"Meet me there in an hour."

NICOLE PUT down her phone and looked out the living room window onto the street. Everything was as it should be. No unusual cars, no movers, no delivery vans, no plumbers or cable company trucks. What could Lily's problem be? That girl needed to toughen up. Nicole went into the kitchen and wrote a note that she left on the counter by the wine they'd opened yesterday: *Love, I'll be back before 7:00. Order some delivery. Surprise me. Nicki.*

She put a red wig into her shoulder bag and put on a hooded jacket. She left out of the condo through the back door, cut through the neighbor's yard and out onto the street behind. She walked two blocks, turned right, walked another block. The streets were quiet. No one was following her. She took out her phone and ordered a rideshare. When the car arrived, she had her hood up. When the traffic got busy, she put on the red wig and pulled the hood up over the wig. The car turned left. "Stop here," she said.

The car pulled over. "You sure?" the driver said. "Your destination is another block."

"This is fine."

She stood on the sidewalk and watched the car drive away. Then she veered off into a small park. Lily was sitting on a bench in the sun. "Walk with me," Nicole said.

Lily told her what had happened. "How can they be sure the video is erased?"

"It's not about the video," Nicole said. "You could destroy it. Let them look at your equipment. It wouldn't make any difference. They'd just have new demands. We're playing a game. The game of who has power over the other players. They make you afraid, they keep you afraid, they don't have to worry about the video getting out. Whoever has power has freedom."

"But how does knowing that help me?"

"Sanders has hired someone. Or someone he trusts has hired someone. Who? How far will they go? What will they do if you don't cooperate? Harass you? Threaten to hurt you? Kill you? Should you kill him first?"

"That's crazy."

"I'm just talking about the absolute limits of a situation like this. You've got your stuff. If Sanders is dead, the video doesn't matter. There's no reason for anyone to pressure you."

"Nicole, look, he's an asshole, okay, but he's a father. Kids are counting on him. I don't want to have anything to do with killing anyone."

"Relax. We're not going to kill him."

"What are we going to do?"

"We need to turn the tables on him. He wants to intimidate you. We need to intimidate him."

"We could release the video."

"Then the game is over. What will he do if you ruin his life? Will he go psycho? Do you want to take that risk?"

"No."

They stopped walking. Nicole continued. "So other than using the video, how do we make him so afraid he'll back off, not just now, but forever? What if someone else had the video? A gang boss. Sanders could pay to have the video destroyed."

"But he still won't know if it's really gone."

"But it wouldn't be personal anymore. And he wouldn't be dealing with you and your limited resources. He'd be dealing with the unknown and all that entails. He wouldn't be able to retaliate. He's just have to live with his fear."

"So we're going to sell the video?"

"I didn't say that."

"Then what are we going to do?"

"I know someone who might be able to help."

"Who?"

"First things first. We're going to buy a new pair of phones. You're not calling my phone or James's landline, and I'm not calling your phone or that other phone you bought. All those phones could already be compromised. Then you're going to sit tight, follow your normal routine. Let me know if you see the bearded guy again. I'll be in touch as soon as I have something to report."

IN THE NIGHT, after Denison went to sleep, Nicole got out of bed, pulled on her robe, and walked through the house looking for her primary phone. She found it in a basket on the kitchen counter. She'd thought about pulling together a crew to do the crime boss impersonation. Maybe she could get Blaxploitation Star to help. Maybe he had a friend. Big black guys would certainly scare the hell out of Sanders. Or she could ask around and scout out a couple of professionals. Less chance of an accident. But Sanders would never believe that she was in charge—he was too sexist for that. And if this project went wrong, if her players overreacted, and Sanders wound up dead or the police ended up in the mix, her little house of cards would come tumbling down. James would be at risk. No. She couldn't have that. Especially since she had told him she wouldn't take any chances. She had to have Tony. She didn't want to make the call. Lily wasn't his problem. She didn't want to put Tony at risk for a no-money gig—all downside and no upside for him, but she couldn't think of any other way. She speed-dialed his number.

"Hey, Mom," he said.

"Were you sleeping?"

"Maybe."

"I need your help."

"Tell me about it."

She could hear him rustling about as if he were getting out of bed. She explained the problem.

"I think you're right," he said. "I think the impersonation is a good call. Give me two days. Find the location for the meet. Set it up as if Lily's going to show, then I'll pull a changeup. It'll be hard looks and intimidation. If it all goes south, we'll put him in the ground, and the cops will be looking for out-of-town muscle."

"Lily won't like that."

"Does she have to know? And don't tell Denison that I'm coming to town. The less he knows, the better."

"Love you."

"Love you too."

TONY WAS STANDING in the dark in the living room, naked, his phone in his hand. The edges of the closed curtains glowed from the street lamp outside. He heard a noise. A plump, middle-aged woman wearing a thin gown, her gray-streaked hair hanging in a braid over one shoulder, appeared in the doorway from the hall. "Something up with your mom?"

He smiled. "Nothing to worry about. She forgets what time it is." He kissed the woman. "I have to go check on her, though. Didn't like the sound of her voice. Want to make sure nothing's wrong at the care center."

She put her arm around him. "You're such a good son."

"Let's go back to bed." He led her back toward the bedroom. "I'll have to leave in the morning. I'll be gone a few days, but I'll be back before you know it."

"We've got tickets for the concert on Saturday."

"I'll be back by Thursday—Friday at the latest. I promise."

ON WEDNESDAY, Tony flew into Oakland International Airport. His ID read C.D. Abbot. He was wearing jeans, Birkenstock sandals, and a battered straw hat. Out on the sidewalk in front of the baggage claim, two men were waiting for him in a stolen Prius. They were big men, crowded into the front seats, one black and one Latino. They were dressed California casual. Tony ducked into the back seat. "Hey, Josh. Hey, Lorenzo. Glad you guys could make it."

Josh, the black one, put the car in drive. "Wouldn't miss it for the world."

"You guys geared up?"

"Always," Lorenzo said. "Almost didn't recognize you, brother."

"We're going up to Berkeley. Got to blend in."

They got on the interstate headed north. "Like I told you before, this is just a salary job. One thousand a day, three days max. If you have to pull a gun, that's an extra grand."

"Easy money," Josh said.

They stopped on the street at the edge of the University of California campus. Tony got out of the car. "I'll be back in thirty minutes, more or less."

He walked up the hill into campus. Students poured out of the buildings: jeans, gym clothes, yoga pants; bikes and skateboards. Nobody paid the least bit of attention to him. Up ahead was a grove of tall conifers. He spotted Nicole sitting on a stone bench under one of the trees. She stood up to hug him. "Missed you," she said.

"Missed you more."

"So you're staying with the Iowa woman?"

"Sybil Anderson. I'm living at her house. It's on a lake outside Kickapoo Creek."

"How are you spinning it?"

"Because of my work, I've always been kind of rootless. Never had kids. Then my wife passed away last year."

"Ouch."

"Widower is always a better sell than being divorced. As you well know, being divorced or never married is like being from the damaged goods section of the discount store. How's Denison?"

"He's fine."

"I bet he is."

She punched him in the shoulder. "Will you stop it?"

He chuckled. "You got the meeting set up?"

"Tomorrow night. Here's the place." She got out her smartphone and pulled up Goggle Maps. "Abandoned industrial zone on the bay. Right here." She pointed it out. "Bad place for an ambush. Easy access to two freeway on-ramps. Last two nights, nobody was near there after eight or nine p.m. The meet is set for eleven. The tide is going out until after two."

"Great. You got Sanders's phone number?"

She gave it to him. "You want me with you?"

"No. You're going to be setting your air-tight alibi. And your girl—Lily? She knows to set her own, right? Separate from yours."

"She's going to be sleeping over at a friend's."

"That'll do. I hope she's worth it. Seems like a lot of trouble for a car that wasn't even stolen. If this goes bad, I could be six thousand out of pocket."

"She's a natural, but it turns out she just doesn't have the stomach for the game."

"Most don't."

"Will I see you after?"

"I'd love that."

Tony walked back down the hill. That old happiness. The electricity. The confidence. Whenever he was with her, he was one step better than he was on his own. That was why he had to call her when he got shot. He could have made do, figured it out, called someone else, but he hadn't wanted to. And it was the same for her. She could have handled this little plot on her own, but she hadn't wanted to. It was an excuse to get together. And grooming up Lily. Teaching her, testing her. Nicole really couldn't keep her hand out of the game. Always scheming. Maybe she was too young to retire. Grifting was all she knew. Maybe Denison was just going to have to wait a few years. She could visit him three or four times a year to keep him on the string and spend the rest of the time with him on the con. He really did miss her.

The Prius was waiting at the curb. He ducked into the back seat and pulled the industrial site up on his phone. "I've got a spot we need to check out." He showed the phone to Lorenzo.

"I know that place. Down past the county park. Take the next left, Josh, then get over to the right."

The battered sign next to the broken gate read Apollo Mechanicals. A newer sign read No Dumping. A dirt path circled through broken slabs of concrete, rusted steel cable, and twisted framing to oversized machinery. Weedy shrubs and tough grasses grew up from hills of earth. Plastic bags, cans, bottles, and broken furniture completed the picture. At the back of the circle, the ground fell away to a sea wall of boulders and concrete pieces and the bay beyond. "Stop here," Tony said.

They got out of the car. "This is the best place for the meet. They'll set up here. The back is clear, so no one can get behind you. The cover to the left and right is sparse—just that junk over there—" Tony pointed to the right—"and those two piles of dirt." He walked to the edge of the sea wall and turned around. "Good view down the path both ways."

Josh leaned back against the Prius. "We playing it straight?"

"Never. Have you got the guns?"

"Picked them up this morning," Lorenzo said. "Got them from an old prison buddy. All old, serial numbers burned off, just like you wanted."

"Great. The only thing left is for me to make the call." Tony took out a burner phone and called Sanders's private number.

"Hello?"

"Sanders?"

"Speaking."

"This is the man who owns your video."

"What?"

"Bet your wife will be just as surprised as I was. A family man like you. Nasty shit."

"What are you talking about?"

"Little girl owed me. Gave me the video to pay her debt. So now you deal with me. The meet is still on for tomorrow night. Bring ten thousand dollars."

"I can't get that kind of money."

"Sure you can."

"I need more time."

"There isn't any more time. Show up or suffer the consequences."

"Five thousand. I can get five thousand."

"By tomorrow night."

"By tomorrow night."

"Same time. Same place. No bullshit."

"I'll have it."

"And Sanders, the little girl belongs to me. You bother her, I bother yours." Tony ended the call.

Josh laughed. "You're as convincing as ever."

"Let's get out of here."

SANDERS SMACKED his fist down on his desk. Jesus Christ. The little minx had sold the video. Why couldn't he catch a break? He picked up his office phone. "Marty? Got a minute? It's urgent."

"Be right up."

He fiddled around with the papers in his inbox until Colvin arrived. "Shut the door," he said.

Colvin settled into the visitor's chair facing Sanders's desk. "What's up?"

Sanders told him about the phone call. "So she didn't even have the video."

"Maybe." Colvin shifted his weight. "You got a call. That's all you know. You don't know if they have the video. You don't know how they got your phone number. Hell, you don't even know if they are *they*. Could be some friend of hers."

Sanders shrugged.

"At this point, would you pay five thousand to get the video and be done with this distraction?"

"Give five thousand to her? No. She created this problem. Besides, we've talked about the copy problem."

"But if it's as advertised?"

"If it's really over? But when is it going to end? This guy wants five thousand. What does the next guy want?"

"You're going to the meet. You can judge for yourself. But you might need to change your approach."

"Meaning?"

"Look, the contractor is the expert. You could let him make the decisions. You pay, you don't pay, he does what he needs to do. Either way, it's all settled tomorrow night."

"I don't know if I want to go that far."

"I didn't get you into this mess. You came to me. Do you want out? You could always let them post the video and deal with the fallout."

"He can make it all go away?"

"Worst-case scenario, the contractor kills this gangster. You think the girl would talk to anyone after that? There's no downside for you."

"Okay. I'll do it."

THURSDAY EVENING, Denison and Nicole were at a cocktail party to raise money for Denison's Bright Horizons job training program for aged-out foster kids. There were a dozen people there who could vouch for them, including two women from the mayor's office. Lily was staying with Chrissie on the pretext that an old boyfriend was bothering her. They'd ordered delivery pizza. Lily had paid, flirted up the delivery guy, and given him a large tip. They picked a movie to watch on Chrissie's smart TV, and Lily paid for it via her Amazon Prime account.

At 11:00 p.m., Tony, Josh, and Lorenzo, now driving a Cadillac Escalade, rolled through the broken gate of Apollo Mechanicals. Tony was dressed in a suit and tie. In his pocket was an empty smartphone with the video on it, which he was going to claim was the original. He slowed the car to a crawl. Josh and Lorenzo slipped out and disappeared into the dark. Tony continued down the dirt path. Up ahead, where he'd predicted, a BMW sat with its headlights on, the light illuminating two dirt piles to the right. A man with a shaved head and a mustache stood beside the BMW with a plastic grocery bag in one hand. Tony pulled up short of the lit-up area, made sure his Glock was loose in its holster, and climbed out.

He called over to the man at the BMW. "Sanders?"

"Yeah."

"Step away from the car."

Sanders took two steps.

Tony started toward him. "I've got something for you." He reached in his jacket pocket and pulled out the smartphone.

A bearded man pointing an assault rifle appeared out of the dark on the left. "That's far enough."

Tony stopped. "So this is how we're playing it?"

"This is exactly how." Sanders snatched the phone from Tony's hand. He found the video and played it. "This is the original?"

Tony nodded.

"Any copies?"

"No."

"Why should I believe you?"

"'Cause I'm a businessman. My word has got to mean something. I tell you I'm selling something, that's what I'm selling."

"What's Lily to you?"

"She owes me. So she belongs to me now. That's all you need to know."

"What if she owes me a debt?"

"Not anymore. That's all done."

The bearded man lowered his rifle. "Pay him."

"Pay him?" Sanders looked at him as if he were crazy.

"Yeah," the bearded man said. "Pay him."

As Sanders reached forward with the bag, Josh came up behind the bearded man and pushed a pistol into his neck. "Easy there, buddy. You've been doing fine so far. Drop the rifle."

Lorenzo came out of the shadows on the right, his pistol also trained on the bearded man. The man set the rifle on the ground.

Sanders's head swiveled from Josh to Lorenzo. Tony dropped into a boxing stance and punched him in the face. He stumbled backward. The bag fell to the ground. Tony hit him again. "I don't like people pointing guns at me."

Lorenzo crossed to Josh and the bearded man, picked up the bearded man's rifle, and whacked him in the temple with the rifle butt. He crumpled to the ground. Josh cuffed his hands behind his back and searched him for other weapons. Lorenzo tossed the assault rifle into the dark.

Tony pulled his Glock and grabbed Sanders by his shirt front. "Get on your knees." He put his gun in Sanders's face.

Sanders sobbed, "Please, please, it's all a misunderstanding. I was afraid. I wasn't sure you'd be straight with me."

"Open your mouth or I'll break out your teeth."

Tony pushed the barrel of the Glock into Sanders's mouth. Sanders screwed his eyes closed. "Bam," Tony said.

Josh and Lorenzo laughed. "Look at that," Lorenzo said, "he pissed himself."

Tony wiped the barrel of his gun off on Sanders's shoulder. "Next time, I pull the trigger." He picked up the plastic bag and ruffled through a wad of hundred-dollar bills. It looked like the $5,000 was all there. "Lily belongs to me. You bother her—even speak to her—I'll come for your kids."

"No," Sanders said. "I understand. I don't want anything to do with her."

"That's a very healthy choice. You stay right where you are until we're gone."

Tony, Josh, and Lorenzo climbed back into the Cadillac, circled around, and drove away. "Thanks, guys," Tony said.

"We pulled guns," Lorenzo said.

"A deal's a deal," Tony said.

"Plus the daily rate," Josh said.

"The job was so easy," Lorenzo said. "I almost feel sorry taking your money. Almost."

"Guys," Tony said, "stop rubbing it in. You're going to get paid."

"Just breaking your balls," Josh said.

11

GOODBYES

Nicole was nursing a sparkling water, pretending it was a vodka soda, while she listened to a retired fruit company executive talk about his ski vacation in the Alps. The sort of high-end destination this guy was talking about was the perfect place to pick up a lot of expensive jewelry in a hurry. But she had to put that out of her mind. James needed a check from this guy for Bright Horizons. He'd been helpful with job-training money in the past—had even helped some youth get summer jobs—but now James needed for him to step up to the next level.

His wife came over and put her hand on his arm. She looked as if the hardest thing she'd ever done was graduate from college. "That's enough, dear," she said. "Our vacation is a lot more interesting to you than it is to Nicole."

"It's fascinating, actually," Nicole replied.

The wife ignored her. "I want you to meet someone." She pulled him away.

Nicole stepped over to the floor-to-ceiling windows and looked out over the city. The view from here was spectacular. The lights on the bridge, the headlights racing along the streets. She wondered how many people stayed in this building over the holidays. The safes alone would probably make the job worthwhile. Her phone vibrated. It was Tony.

"All done," he said.

"Have you got him on the straight and narrow?"

"He won't be making any more trouble."

"Great. Where are you?"

"I'm on my way to the Marriott by the airport."

"Oakland?"

"Yeah."

"I'll be there as soon as I can."

When Nicole found Denison, he was talking with Jill, the director of his foundation, and one of the young women from the mayor's office. She put her hand on his back and leaned up to his ear. "I have to go," she whispered.

He smiled and nodded.

"I'll see you at home."

He turned and kissed her.

She ordered a rideshare before she got on the elevator. She only had to wait at the corner for a few minutes before a Camry pulled up.

"You're going to the Marriott in Oakland?"

"Yes."

The car merged into the night traffic. Nicole got out her extra phone to call Lily. "Hey. Can you talk?"

"Just a minute."

The Camry bumped down the street and took a quick left.

"Okay," Lily said.

"It's all taken care of."

"You're sure?"

"He won't bother you anymore."

"But he's not..."

"No, he was just made to see reason," Nicole said.

"How?"

"We're not going to get into that."

"But it's done?"

"Yes."

"Thank you."

"So it's the straight and narrow for you?"

"It's—I really, really, really appreciate what you've done for me. But I just can't do that stuff anymore."

"I understand."

AT THE MARRIOTT, Tony and Nicole were lying together on the bed. The lights were on. Their clothes were scattered across the carpet. The curtain to the balcony was open, showing the night sky. Tony leaned up on one elbow so that he could look at her. "Paid the guys four apiece, so I'm three grand out of pocket."

"You sure about Sanders?"

"Guy peed his pants. His backup guy—some merc from a legit armed-response company, I'm going to guess—didn't even resist."

"I missed you," she said.

He squeezed her shoulder. "It's been too long." He glanced at the clock. "Do you have to go back tonight?"

"I've got another hour to get my story straight."

"But he knows about us?"

"Yeah, I always tell him the truth. But this is his world, so it's sort of cheating."

He smiled. "Makes the sex even better, doesn't it?"

She ran her hand along his side. "Almost all healed. The scar will be even smaller than the other one."

"Shot twice in that side. Both times it was from jumping the gun. You weren't there to make me think it through. I rely on you too much."

"Too much?"

"If you're not standing beside me." He took her hand in his. "I know I said I was cool with Denison, that he could be your retirement plan, but I don't want you to think I'm pushing you away."

"What are you saying?"

"You're always my girl. You know that, right?"

"I know it."

"So if you don't think you can play the straight game, if you think you're too young or it's just too hard, you know you're not trapped—"

She poked him in the ribs. "You want me to come back to you."

"I'm just saying—"

"You need me. You need me as much as I need you. Why don't you just admit it? We both know it."

"Look—"

She kissed him. "You're so sweet when you're trying to be honest. But I have less than an hour left, and all this honesty is making me horny. So stop talking."

Afterward, Tony watched as she washed up and got dressed. "To continue our conversation," she said while she looked in the bathroom mirror, combing her hair. "You don't want to tell me what to do, but if I'm fed up with the straight life, you want me back."

"It's a lot of money to give up. Originally, I saw it as sort of a long-term con, but now I know that's not the way it works. And the way we click together. It's just special."

She put down her brush. "Yeah, it is special. And it is a lot of money. But money has never been a problem for us. Not for long."

"Maybe you could go visit him five or six times a year."

She got out her makeup to touch up her face. "He already thinks he's agreeing to too much. I'm sure I could come visit until he found a new woman, but the future Mrs. Denisons are already circling."

"If you stay here, there's no more extracurricular for you."

"Yeah, it really is all or nothing. If I stay with him, I'm eventually going to have to agree to marry him, and then he won't want me working with you at all."

"Full retirement."

"Full retirement. I don't know if I'll ever be ready."

"I'll put you on my Christmas card list."

"Don't be a bastard."

In the elevator on the way down, she gave herself the hard look-over in the mirror. Her hair, her makeup, her clothes all looked the same as when she had left Denison at the fund-raiser. Maybe she'd get lucky and he'd be asleep when she got home.

It was 2:30 a.m. when the rideshare dropped her off at the door to the condo. The lights were on. She found Denison standing in the living room still dressed from the party, a glass of whiskey in his hand. "Well?"

"All settled." She kicked off her shoes.

"And?"

"Nobody's dead. Sanders is going to leave Lily alone."

"Who did you go see tonight? Nothing bad happened, so you can tell me."

"Tony."

"He's been in town?"

"I called him when things got out of hand. I promised you I wouldn't take any chances, so I didn't."

"You got Tony to take them."

She poured herself a whiskey.

"How long has he been here?"

"A couple of days. He'll be gone tomorrow. The guys he hired have already left."

"What did he do?"

"James, I'm not telling you that. No one was injured. That's all you need to know." She started toward the hallway. "You coming to bed?"

She led the way to the bedroom. She set her drink on her dresser, stripped off her dress, and went into the bathroom in her underwear. She turned on the shower. "Do you have to get up in the morning?"

"No."

She was in the shower when Denison entered the bathroom. "Come on in," she said.

He climbed into the shower. She could smell the whiskey on him. She put her hands on his hips. "How much have you had to drink?"

"Enough."

She kissed him. "You're not a drinker. What's worrying you?"

"All this business. You sneaking around. Lily. I figured Tony was in town. You act a little different when he's nearby. It's that world from the kidnapping. I love you, but I can't live in a world where I don't know what's true and what's not."

"But you know what's true right now. Me and you, together. Tomorrow doesn't come until tomorrow." She kissed him again. "Take your shower."

She was in bed in the dark when he came back into the bedroom. She saw his naked silhouette before he turned off the bathroom light. "You don't want to make a girl wait too long."

He climbed into bed. "I don't know if I'm up for this."

She remembered the first time, how awkward and honest he'd been, no guile in him at all, his sadness about his newly dead wife, his appreciation as if she'd been performing a repulsive task, fucking a bad-smelling mark, not making love to a handsome, gentle man. Making him love her had been too easy. But things were in transition now. Playing the honesty game, she was losing her hold over him. Would she win him back, or was their relationship already on the decline? She knew in her heart that she could never give up Tony. And she knew she wasn't ready to give up Denison. Even though it would have to happen someday, right now, in this moment, she intended to make their relationship as real is it could possibly be. She was going to make love to him tonight, make love to him so deeply that no matter what happened in the future, whenever he thought of her, he'd be thinking of them locked together in ecstasy. That would be her gift to him.

The day was already bright when Nicole finally woke up. Denison was still asleep, his face turned away from her. She slipped on her robe, waved at the housekeeper who was dusting in the living room, and padded into the kitchen, where she made coffee. When she returned to the bedroom with two cups, Denison was awake. He sat up in bed, squinting in the light. "My head is pounding." Nicole took two ibuprofen out of the pocket of her robe and handed them to him. "Thanks," he said. "I should have taken them last night."

"You shouldn't have drunk so much. You're a brooder. Drinking just makes you brood more."

"I don't know if I've ever liked the cheerful morning you."

She sat on the edge of the bed. "What about the cheerful afternoon me? Or the cheerful evening me?"

"I just got really worried. We agreed to compartmentalize—we're here in our compartment, then you've got your other compartments when you're not here, but I can't always keep my head in this compartment. The unknown can lead to a bad emotional place."

"I didn't help by playing hooky with Lily. I'm going to try harder to be here when I'm here—not just hanging around, but having a real life. I've just got to decide what that life is going to be, how I'm going to model it, and I've been putting that off."

"Why not just be yourself? That's who I love."

"Jimmy, myself is exactly what you don't want me to be."

He looked at her quizzically.

"Here, with you, you want my personality but not my inclinations."

"That's not true."

"Being on the con is not something I learned to do because I needed to make money and I couldn't do anything else—well, maybe it was for a little while, but that was a long time ago. Being on the con is who I am. Doing the straight life, for me, is setting up a con that I'm never going to spring. Convincing everyone that I'm trustworthy so they'll let their guard down and then not taking anything. It's like quitting smoking and always walking around with an unlit cigarette in your hand. Does that make sense? It's like you going around acting like you're going to help people and then not helping them. Could you do that?"

"So how can you ever know if you're really being honest with anyone?"

"You don't have to be disinterested to be honest. You were honest with the people at the fund-raiser, weren't you? Even if you called it a cocktail party. Even if we were setting our alibi."

"But I didn't lie to them."

"But you were trading on their emotions, their friendship, their desire to be thought of as generous."

"For a good cause."

"Because you get to decide what's good?"

"But what about in our relationship?"

"I'm on the con. I'm honest with you because I want you to really love me, no matter what I do. Working so far?"

"I hadn't thought about it that way."

"It's the same for you, isn't it? You're hoping to keep my love. And when you get jealous," she smiled, "is when you're afraid you're not inside the game anymore."

"I don't want it to be a game. It's got to be more than that."

"Jimmy, I promise you, I'm always going to tell you everything."

"What about Tony?"

"What about him?"

"Did you sleep with him while he was here?"

"Yes."

"I thought so. So when he's here, there are no compartments."

"Yeah, I guess it's true."

"I don't think I can accept that. Sharing you in another world is not the same as sharing you here."

"I don't want to hurt you."

"Then don't hurt me. Be with me or be with him. Make up your mind."

12

LOOSE ENDS

On Labor Day, in Albuquerque, New Mexico, at two o'clock in the morning, Tony and Nicole were waiting in the shadows by the steel door to a high-security storage unit while Alphonso, their computer guy, was bypassing the alarms and motion sensors. "I still have a hard time believing that the money is here," Nicole said.

"If the info is good, one hundred K in small bills," Tony said.

"I think it's all bullshit."

"We'll see in a minute."

"All set, boss," Alphonso said.

Tony picked the locks and pulled open the door. Three duffel bags sat on a wire shelf mounted to the back wall. Tony opened the closest bag. It was crammed full of twenties, tens, and fives. Drug money.

"Don't they count this shit?" Alphonso asked.

"They weigh it," Tony said. "They know how it averages out."

The other bags were the same. They loaded them into their stolen Ford, closed the door to the storage unit, and reset the alarm system. Nicole slid in behind the wheel. She took a left out of the storage facility and then a right onto Jackson Boulevard.

"Hey," Alphonso said, "I thought we were going back to the motel."

"Never go back," Tony said. "That's where the bushwhackers or the police are waiting." He turned in his seat and pointed his pistol at Alphonso's chest. "If you move your hands, I'm going to think you're reaching for your gun."

"You got me wrong, boss. I'm not the guy who cheats his partners."

Tony shook his head. "There's always one on every crew, isn't there, baby?"

"Yeah," Nicole replied, "somebody who thinks they're smarter than anyone else."

She pulled up an alley behind a pizzeria and parked next to the dumpster. The air smelled of burned crust and rotting vegetables.

Tony gestured with his gun. "So which are you, Alphonso: double-crosser or cop?"

Alphonso's eyes had the deer-in-the-headlights look.

Nicole got out of the driver's seat holding a sawed-off shotgun and opened the back seat door next to Alphonso. "Out you go. Don't make me shoot you." She grabbed him by the collar, pushed the shotgun into his side, and pulled him out of the car.

Tony came around the car, pushed Alphonso up against the fender, frisked him, and took his pistol. "Let me make it easy for you, Detective. I think you're a task-force cop, wife and two kids waiting at home. You prove you're a cop, you walk away."

"I'm not an asshole, and I'm not a cop."

Tony smacked him in the back of the head. "Listen up. There is no third choice. There's only two. Die here or walk away. What's it going to be?"

"My ID's inside my left shoe."

"Kick them off."

Under the insole of his left shoe was a state police ID. Tony smiled. "You just saved your life, my friend. Don't screw this up. We're taking the money and leaving. You're going home to your family."

They cuffed his hands with plastic cuffs, pushed him down onto the back seat, and cuffed his ankles. They pulled the duffels from the trunk, walked down the alley to a black RAV4 parked beside the service entrance to another store, put the bags in the back, and circled around onto Jackson Boulevard. "You were right about Alphonso," Tony said.

"We both knew there was something about him that didn't add up."

"Yeah, but I thought he was going to rip us off."

"It's better this way."

"Yeah. Always better when they don't know who you are and you don't have to kill them."

Nicole took the ramp onto the freeway. "We'll be at the airport in two hours."

"When's your flight?"

"Six a.m."

"Did Denison call at all this time?"

"No. Like I told you, he's not worried anymore. He's conflicted. He's still grateful that I saved Bell from that psycho and he's still in love with me, but he's jealous of my relationship with you and angry that I won't stop helping you."

"You going to turn on the charm?"

"After all the honesty, it would be hard to fool him. I know I could do it. I just don't have the heart. He's not just another mark. I'm not going to rob him, so what's the point?"

"So it's crash and burn?"

"You ever wonder, baby, how it is that people do these relationships? They fool themselves, and they see what they want to see."

"Sybil's doing a great job. This is my third visit to see my mom at the care center, and she hasn't asked if she can come with me."

"You've always been a wonderful son."

"Thanks."

She sped up to pass a semitruck before they started up a hill. "But you don't love her."

"No. But I enjoy her company. She's under my protection. I wouldn't hurt her or let anyone else hurt her."

"Do you know when you'll leave her?"

"I can't stay forever, but I'm hiding in plain sight. I've got no reason to go. Unless you're wanting to make a change."

"Retirement. It was a great idea. A wonderful gift."

"Thanks."

"And I do love Jimmy. But I'm not in love with him. I've only ever been in love with you."

"It's just us, honey. Me and you against the world. Skin on skin. No matter where you are."

"So it's not really retirement if I'm not spending it with you."

"But you're going back?"

"For now. I owe Jimmy a smooth exit."

"You are one classy lady."

"Stop it. You need time to finish things off with Sybil anyway. And then there's that little project you're planning. You think this is enough money?"

"One hundred grand in untraceable bills? Definitely. Robertson is going to wish he never met me."

IN DECEMBER, Paul Robertson was in Colorado, standing with Vishnu Industries's security director outside the chain-link fence surrounding their research campus. A light snow was whipping around in the wind. His hands were in his overcoat pockets. There was a hole cut in the fence and multiple tracks in the snow leading into the woods.

The security director, a black man wearing a military-style parka, rubbed his hands together to warm them. "Our guys followed the tracks through the woods to the state highway. Looks like there was a vehicle parked on the side of the road."

"Anyone notice it?"

"Road is quiet at night. Sheriffs only come through one time on patrol. We've seen the surveillance footage from the Stop N Go to the north and Grady's Gas to the south, but it's all locals."

"Won't matter. It's all bullshit. I still think our forensics team will find that someone hacked the computers, stole the code and the records without even coming on site."

"You think you can track them?"

"We'll do our best. But it's a dangerous world. Hackers are always testing systems, looking for low-hanging fruit. If you want to avoid problems in the future, you need a security upgrade."

"So this is the pitch?"

Robertson shrugged. "The main office will be in touch."

They shook hands. Robertson got into his rented Ford Explorer, turned on the heated seat, and drove back around the perimeter to the access road. He still had time to drive to Denver today. He'd be back in Washington, DC, tomorrow evening in time to take Martha to dinner at the Thai place she liked. He should have moved to the private sector a long time ago. Twice the pay and half the hours.

On his way down the canyon, he decided to pull into a Travel Ace truck stop to eat dinner. The night had come on, and the snow was heavy now. Fat wet flakes covered the windshield just as fast at the wipers could clear them off. The front parking was full, so he had to park around the side of the building. He climbed out of the truck into the muddy slush and made his way inside.

TONY, driving a stolen utility van, was following Robertson down the canyon. When he pulled into the Travel Ace, Tony pulled in behind him and stopped at the outside of the parking lot where he watched Robertson park and go inside. Then he parked in the spot next to Robertson's Explorer. He pulled up the hood on his parka, went into the truck stop, and glanced up and down the aisles of the convenience store, but no Robertson. He looked into the restaurant. Robertson was sitting at a table looking in a menu. Tony smiled. Perfect. He went back outside. The wind was driving the snow horizontally across the lot. People had their heads down, hurrying to get inside or into their cars. He stepped into the space between the Explorer and the utility van, lay down in the slush, and slid under the SUV. He used a penlight to find the brake line and cut into it with a pipe cutter until the brake fluid was leaking at a steady drip. By the time he slid out from under the truck and got to his feet, his pants legs and his left shoulder were sopping and his teeth were chattering. He stomped around for a few minutes in hopes of knocking some of the slush off the back of his parka. Then he got into the van, turned up the heat, and moved to a spot where he'd be able to follow the Explorer when it left.

Twenty minutes later, Tony watched Robertson come out the truck stop with a to-go coffee, get in the Explorer, and continue on his way. Tony pulled out after him. The roadway was slick, and there were a lot of cars on the canyon road, their headlights bobbing in the snowy gloom. His wipers were icing up. He pushed the heater to Defrost and the fan up to High. Some cars were creeping along, others were barreling down the road and passing at every opportunity. Tony was right behind Robertson, but he wasn't worried about being spotted. He watched Robertson tap his brakes as he came up on an old pickup truck. A Suburban blew past all three of them, throwing slush as it flew by.

A sign indicated switchbacks. The road began to snake. The ravine on the right was a black hole. Robertson was tapping the Explorer's brakes, but it didn't seem to make any difference to its speed. The pickup truck slid to the right. The driver steered against the slide. The back end of the pickup truck swished from side to side but straightened out. The pickup truck eased toward the middle of the road as if the driver couldn't tell where the outer edge of the road was. A semitruck was huffing up the road toward them. It sounded its horn. The pickup began to ease over into its own lane, but the Explorer was moving too fast, its brake lights burning red. It veered right to miss hitting the pickup, but it didn't veer enough. Its left front end clipped the right back bumper of the pickup, causing it to bounce into the oncoming lane. The Explorer spun sideways and disappeared into the ravine. The semitruck, horn blaring, smashed the left front of the pickup and dragged it up the canyon.

Tony swerved around the truck, managing to keep two wheels on the road. Then he put on his flashers and pulled over onto the right of way. He got out the passenger's side of the van and walked back to the point where the Explorer had left the road. The traffic crawled past the wrecked pickup and semi. Across the way, the truck driver, in coveralls and a cowboy hat, was setting out road flares. Tony looked down into the ravine, but he couldn't see anything. He couldn't tell how steep the grade was or how far down the Explorer was or how many pieces it was in. And he wasn't going to screw up this beautiful accident by crawling down there to put a bullet in Robertson's head. How many people were even aware that the Explorer had gone off the road? It could sit down there until spring.

He trudged back to the van, flipped on his turn signal, and waited for a long gap in the traffic before he eased back on the road and continued down the canyon to the deserted parking lot where he'd left his Cadillac Escalade. It was still there. He turned it on and scraped the snow off the windows. Then he poured a five-gallon can of gas over the inside of the utility van, pulled off his parka and tossed it in the van, and set the van on fire. The fire was roaring inside the van as he pulled out of the parking lot and drove back to his motel. It was a good night to watch TV and order some pizza.

TWO DAYS LATER, Tony was traveling the interstate south from Minneapolis. A storm had blown through the day before, leaving five inches of snow in its wake, and the snowplows had piled the snow deep onto the sides of the road. Just as Tony was entering the interchange east of Kickapoo Creek, he got a call on his smartphone, which he took via the interface in the Escalade. He didn't know the number of the caller, but no one knew this number, so his interest was piqued. "Hello?"

"You know who this is?"

It was Garcia's voice. "Yes."

"I know you did it."

"What are you talking about?"

"Robertson."

"I don't have the slightest idea where he is."

"When you lie, you are even more convincing than when you tell the truth. That's your tell."

"What's this about?"

"I had to be sure I was right." She ended the call.

Tony got that spooky feeling that someone was watching him that he couldn't see. He exited the interstate downtown, drove up to city hall, back down to the county courthouse, and over the bridge headed toward the airport. No one was following him. He continued south of town through the snow-covered corn stubble until he came to a gated community situated next to a lake. The gate opened when he rolled up. He meandered down the winding streets, the driveways scraped clean and the extra snow piled into hills at the end of the cul-de-sacs. Up ahead on the left was Sybil's house. But something wasn't right. A red Sentra was parked in her driveway. He drove on by without slowing down and continued up the hill to the clubhouse, where he pulled into a parking spot with a good view of the street and called Sybil.

"Syb? It's C.D."

"Where are you? I thought you'd be home by now."

"I got a late start out of the Twin Cities this morning. And there was a fender bender just this side of the Iowa border."

"But you're okay?"

"Yeah, I'm fine. Didn't want you to worry. That's why I called. I should be there in an hour. Do you want to go out to eat?"

"I'm already cooking."

"Super. See you in an hour." He ended the call.

I'm already cooking. No one who knew her would believe that. But maybe she really was cooking. Maybe he was just being paranoid. Maybe Garcia was testing him. Maybe she figured that if he ran, he must be guilty. She couldn't go after him for Robertson. She didn't want that government-sponsored crime spree out in the open. That had congressional oversight committee written all over it. No, she was messing with his head, pure and simple. All he had to do was keep his cool.

He waited forty-five minutes and then drove back to Sybil's house.

The Sentra was still in her driveway. He parked beside it and went in the front door.

"There you are!" Sybil came into the front hall from the kitchen. She had an apron on over her dress. "It's about time you got here. Your friend has been here over an hour." She kissed him. "We're in the kitchen."

He hung up his overcoat and moved his Glock into the pocket of his suit jacket. He didn't want to kill anyone in Sybil's house, and he wasn't sure if their relationship was strong enough for him to sell it to her afterward, but if Garcia had sent someone to kill him, he wouldn't have any other choice.

He went into the kitchen. Garcia, wearing her usual black pantsuit, was standing at the granite counter, a cutting board covered with chopped vegetables in front of her. The knife was in easy reach.

"Clara," Tony said. "What a surprise." He squeezed her shoulder and kissed her cheek.

She smiled. "I had some business in town. It finished up early, and I remembered that you were here."

Sybil put a covered casserole on the stove top and closed the oven door. "I didn't even know you'd told your work friends about us."

"C.D.'s a private sort of guy," Garcia said. "But when you get to know him, he really opens up."

Sybil glanced from Garcia to Tony. "You security consultants and your privacy. I've been pumping Clara for an hour, and I haven't learned anything."

"I'm sorry," Garcia said. "It's an occupational hazard. Easiest way not to tell a secret accidentally." She turned to Tony. "I've got something for you out in the car. Why don't you walk with me?"

They walked out into the evening cold. The outside lights were on, but the street was deserted and silent in the way heavy snow nights were. Tony put his hand in his jacket pocket. Garcia pressed the Sentra's fob to unlock it. "Get in."

They sat in the front seat. Tony was looking at Garcia's face, but he was concentrating on her hands. If she went for her gun, he was going to kill her, right there in the driveway. He didn't care how many neighbors heard or how many opened their doors to see what was going on. Being identified was always better than being dead.

"Robertson is alive," she said. "I know that's got to hurt."

Tony started to speak.

"Don't bother to deny it. Got a picture of you off a security camera at a Denver motel. There's just too many to avoid them all anymore."

"So where does that leave us?"

"You had your chance. You're done. You leave him be, or I'll hound you off the face of the earth."

"And you're here to prove you can find me whenever you want."

She nodded. "You're a smart guy. Act smart. Fuck this woman and plan your next score in the peace and quiet."

"No disrespect intended," Tony said. "It's just hard to let someone off the hook after they've murdered your partners. Maybe I overstepped my bounds just a little bit. Let bygones be bygones?"

"If you're done with Robertson."

They shook hands.

"We better get back in," Tony said. "Or Sybil will think we're out here smooching."

Later, after Garcia left, Tony wiped down the kitchen counters while Sybil loaded the dishwasher. "You really went above and beyond," Tony said. "You didn't have to cook."

"I wanted to," she replied. "That's the first time I ever met one of your friends."

As she shut the door to the dishwasher, Tony came up behind her, put his arms around her, and kissed her neck. She turned in his arms and kissed him back. "There was something about her. Something guarded, know what I mean?"

"She just lost a friend. She feels responsible. That's what we were talking about outside."

"Killed at work?"

"Yeah. Guy with a wife and kids—grown kids, but still."

"You don't do anything that dangerous?"

"Sometimes. Sometimes you don't know how dangerous a situation is until you're already in it. That's when it's risky."

"I hope you're never in a situation like that again."

"Me too."

She kissed him again. "Come to bed."

"In a minute. I need to make a call."

She gave him a look that said, "You better not be long." He went out into the garage, shut the door, and called Nicole on his backup phone. "Can you talk?"

"I've got a minute."

"Garcia found me. Robertson's still alive. She warned me off him. I'm dumping this phone. You still got the phone we bought at the Save-U-Mart?"

"Yeah."

"I'll call you on that."

"You done with Robertson?"

"Yeah. Garcia's got too many resources."

"So you're on the run?"

"I'm not saying anything else on this phone. Goodbye."

Tony bolted the garage door as he went inside, checked the locks on the patio door and the front door, and kicked off his shoes in the hall before he padded back to the bedroom. He'd been hoping to stay with Sybil until after the holidays, but now he was going to have to disappear. It was a shame to leave her alone at Christmas, but it couldn't be helped. He wasn't safe here anymore, and she wasn't safe with him.

Candles on the dresser lit the bedroom, the light reflecting from the mirror. Sybil lay in bed, her hair loose around her shoulders, the covers pulled up under her arms.

"I thought you'd be too tired," Tony said.

"I'm not through with you yet."

Tony took off his clothes in the dark by an armchair and palmed his Glock. If Garcia sent someone to kill him, tonight would be the night. As he got to his side of the bed, he knelt and laid his Glock on the carpet underneath it.

"What are you doing?" Sybil murmured.

"Thought I felt something with my foot. I was wrong."

He slipped in beside her and ran his hand along her naked torso. He could feel her heavy socks rub against his legs. "Socks? Really?"

"It's freezing."

He smiled. "Not for long."

THE NEXT MORNING, Nicole woke up early. It was still dark. She could have tried to go back to sleep, but she didn't want to. She knew that life was changing, that she was never going to make James truly happy, that there was no reason to drag things out anymore, that she was going to go back to being her true self full time. She got out of bed, leaving Denison to sleep. She eased open the door to her closet so that the hinge wouldn't creak and found her go bag pushed back into the corner. She dragged it out, felt inside for the Save-U-Mart phone, and then carried the bag out into the hall, making sure to close the door as quietly as possible. The phone battery was dead. She padded down the hall to the kitchen, tossed the bag onto the counter, found the charger, and plugged in the phone. While it was charging, she made coffee.

Two hours' time difference. Tony would be up by now. She sat on a stool with her coffee in front of her and the phone in her hand. Was she really going to do it? Was she really going to give up this cushy life? Truth was, she could probably hang on indefinitely: James being disappointed now and again, wanting her to change, her giving him his way just enough of the time to keep hope alive. But why should she when her good life was out there waiting for her? When her man, the one who never bored her, the one who always had her back, the one who—love wasn't even a strong enough word. They were bound together in their deepest places by everything they'd done together. She speed-dialed the number. It rang over and over. She hung up. Drank her coffee. Listened to the morning traffic. Her phone rang.

"Yeah?" Tony asked.

"Remember that Christmas we did that resort in Hawaii?"

Tony chuckled. "That was a good time."

"Meet me in LA on Friday."

"You ready for a new name?"

"Yeah. I'll never be Nicole again."

"I'll get the paperwork lined up. I think there's still a guy in Omaha who makes the good stuff. Any name you'd prefer?"

"You choose."

"Love you."

"Love you."

She slipped back into the bedroom, pulled her nightgown off over her head, and slid back into bed. Denison was lying in his back, his mouth slightly open, his face peaceful. He was a good man. It would be hard for him, but it was for the best. Sometimes, over the last few years, she hadn't really known what she'd wanted—she'd felt like she needed to change, to make her life somehow easier. But now she knew that she never would. The straight life just wasn't going to fill her up. Traveling, grifting, the thrill of the hunt, being always with her one true love no matter what happened—that was the life she was meant for. All that was left was to leave this world behind.

"Hey, sleepyhead."

Denison's eyes fluttered and opened. He smiled. She rolled on top of him and kissed him. She was going to take her time saying goodbye.

A NOTE FROM THE AUTHOR

Thanks for reading *The Murder Run*. If you enjoyed it, please post a review on a review site of your choice. A few words will do. Honest reviews are the number one way I attract new readers. Thanks so much.

I'd love to hear from you. You can reach me at my website: https://michaelpking.org

The Travelers
The Double Cross: A Travelers Prequel
The Traveling Man: Book One
The Computer Heist: Book Two
The Blackmail Photos: Book Three
The Freeport Robbery: Book Four
The Kidnap Victim: Book Five
The Murder Run: Book Six